The
King's Book

Books by Louise A. Vernon

The
King's Book

Louise A. Vernon
Illustrated by Allan Eitzen

Herald
Press

Scottdale, Pennsylvania
Waterloo, Ontario

Library of Congress Cataloging-in-Publication Data

Vernon, Louise A.
  The King's Book.

  SUMMARY: When his father, one of the translators
working on the King James Bible, is accused of treason,
Nat finds himself involved in a series of baffling
incidents as he attempts to discover the identity of
his father's enemy.
  [1. Bible—History—Fiction. 2. England—Fiction]
I. Eitzen, Allan, ill. II. Title.
PZ7.V598Ki   [Fic]   80-18998
ISBN 0-8361-1933-9 (pbk.)

The paper used in this publication is recycled and meets the minimum require-
ments of American National Standard for Information Sciences—Permanence of
Paper for Printed Library Materials, ANSI Z39.48-1984.

To order or request information, please call
1-800-759-4447 (individuals); 1-800-245-7894 (trade).
Website: www.mph.org

My deepest thanks to
Geta Sanderson,
librarian, Bingley College,
Bingley, West Yorkshire, England,
whose skill in research made my
hours in the reading room of
the British Museum
most enjoyable.

CONTENTS

1

SECRET ENEMY

A stone crashed through the front window of a parish house near a small church in London. Nat Culver jumped up from his Hebrew lesson and headed for the door. His mother stopped him.

"Our second week here and there's trouble already," she exclaimed.

"Probably the neighborhood children, Mother. Just an accident."

"Accident?" Mother stepped over the broken glass

and closed the shutters. "Nathaniel, you mustn't be so gullible. We're living in the city now, not the country. Take nothing for granted. Besides, you know how outspoken your father is about the possibility of a Catholic uprising. Maybe there is a secret Catholic in our church. Be that as it may, I know that stone was thrown on purpose."

"I'll find out." Nat ran outside.

A small boy broke away from a group of children playing nearby and ran toward Nat with cap outstretched. "Penny for the guy. Penny for the guy."

"Come back," the others called. "We already have the gunpowder."

Nat caught the boy by the shoulder. "Did you throw that stone through our window?"

The boy wriggled free. "No, I didn't." He scurried back to the other children.

Nat glared at them. "Well, then, which of you did?"

"None of us," one muttered in a sullen voice.

The boy who had begged for a penny blurted out, "We're going to blow you up tomorrow."

"What!" For a moment Nat could not believe he had heard right. Then he remembered Guy Fawkes' Day. Boys spent their pennies for black gunpowder to explode in memory of the Gunpowder Plot, when Catholic traitors had tried to blow up King James.

"I'm not a traitor." Nat could not help smiling at the earnestness of the small boy.

"Your father is. That man told us so, and he's going to give us more money tomorrow."

"Sssssh!" the others hissed. "He told us not to tell."

"And your father is something else, too," the small boy insisted, "but I forget the word."

"Recusant," another said.

10

Nat clenched his fists. The word *recusant* stung. Recusants were people, usually Catholics, who refused to attend the Church of England. When caught, recusants were fined, imprisoned, or both. Why would anyone accuse Father, the rector of a church, and one of the fifty-four learned men of England chosen by King James to revise the Bible? True, Father was the last on the list, a replacement for a translator who had died. There had always been a mystery about Father's not being among the first of the translators. Perhaps his outspokenness had been held against him. Still, words did not do as much harm as stones.

Nat went back into the house. His mother, white-faced, handed him a crumpled piece of paper. "I found this on the floor. It must have been wrapped around the stone. What can it possibly mean?"

Nat smoothed out the paper. " 'Traitor, withdraw, lest worse befall,' " he read aloud. A prickle of fear ran up his spine. Traitors were executed with hundreds of people watching. Nat had heard Father speak of the execution of a Catholic priest, one of over a hundred priests who had been trained abroad and who had returned to England to make secret converts to Catholicism.

But Father was not a Catholic, not a recusant, nor disloyal to his country. Of what was he being accused?

Several sharp explosions sounded outside. Mother gasped, "What's that?"

"It's just gunpowder the children are setting off."

"But whatever for?"

"It's Guy Fawkes' Day tomorrow."

Mother sighed. "November fifth. How could I have forgotten? We were so busy settling in that it slipped my mind." She sat at the table, spread the note out, and ran her hands over it again and again. "To think that the name *Guy Fawkes* will be remembered forever. A traitor to England. What a monstrous deed he did in the name of the Catholics, trying to blow up King James and Parliament, too. And that Thomas Percy, bringing his noble family to shame."

At the name *Percy*, Nat shouted, "That's it! That's it! Wasn't Father in Paris the year before the Gunpowder Plot?"

"Yes. He was searching for the St. Chrysostom manuscripts that Sir Henry Savile wanted."

Nat had always felt sorry for Sir Henry, one of the Bible translators. After the death of his only son, about Nat's age, Sir Henry vowed to spend his entire fortune, if necessary, to publish the writings of St. Chrysostom, a famous Greek church father who had been dead for over a thousand years.

"Didn't Father tell us that he prayed at the sickbed of Henry Percy?"

"Yes," Mother said, "but it was Thomas Percy, a relative, who was one of the gunpowder plotters."

"But don't you see? Someone must think that anyone connected with the Percy family is a traitor." Who was that man who paid the neighborhood children to call Father a recusant? Did he think Father was going to start another Gunpowder Plot? Just being accused meant Father could be arrested and thrown in jail. To be called traitor was worse. It could mean death. Who was Father's secret enemy?

Mother thrust the note into Nat's hands. "Your father must be warned. Give him this note."

"Is he at Sir Dudley's?" Sir Dudley Carleton, son-in-law of Sir Henry Savile, was helping with the St. Chrysostom papers.

"No," Mother said. "He's at Stationers' Hall with the translators."

With the note inside his shirt, Nat soon came to St. Paul's churchyard. On all sides people gossiped and traded. Several small boys, led by a tall, redheaded boy dressed in blue, pushed through the crowd toward the cathedral steps. They heaped gunpowder in small piles and touched them with fire-tipped sticks. Each explosion brought forth comments and laughter from the onlookers.

A church warden flung open the doors of the cathedral and raged at the boys. "What mischief here is afoot? Begone. Let honest folk be about their business."

The redheaded boy protested, "But this is in honor of King James. Have you forgotten Guy Fawkes' Day tomorrow?" He tossed his feathered cap in the air. "Down with Guy Fawkes! Down with gunpowder plotters! Down with all traitors to England, especially Catholics."

The onlookers cheered. The church warden's surliness changed into good humor. "Well spoken indeed, young sir. I see you are a page, and I daresay you will go far at court. Nevertheless, do your celebrating in the churchyard, not on the cathedral steps."

With a mocking salute to the warden, the redheaded boy led the other boys to a far corner of the churchyard. People drifted back to their trading. Nat noticed two men talking earnestly. He recognized Sir Dudley Carleton's secretary, James Collier, a lean, dark-haired man with thin lips and intense gaze. His companion, shorter and stockier, held out both hands in a gesture of pleading.

"But of course I can. Never fear. I know my trade," Nat heard the shorter man say.

Two housewives nearby nudged each other. "There's one of those actor fellows," one said.

The other housewife sniffed. "They shouldn't be allowed to clutter up the churchyard. Pretending to be someone they aren't, in those wicked theaters. It's a wonder God doesn't strike them down."

Nat lingered a while. The talking and laughing excited him. So this was life in London! Far different from the quiet countryside he was used to. He saw Sir Dudley's secretary, James Collier, shake off the restraining hand of the man he was talking to. Somehow, that gesture reminded Nat of his own errand. He hurried down a side street toward Stationers' Hall.

Without knowing why, Nat looked over his shoulder several times. He felt uneasy, as if someone were watching him. Was he being followed? Nat turned down the alley to Stationers' Hall and waited. For what? He did not know. In a moment the redhaired boy he had seen before darted into the alley.

"Were you following me?" Nat looked the boy up and down from the feathered cap, slanted across one eyebrow, the short blue cape flung over one shoulder, and the long blue hose ending in mudstreaked shoes.

"I've been trying to catch up with you to tell you something," the other boy panted.

Nat's thoughts churned. Had this boy thrown the stone through the parish house window? He had a know-it-all manner that rubbed Nat the wrong way. Perhaps he was a page boy for some nobleman.

"A man was following you," the page boy went on. "Probably a pickpocket. St. Paul's churchyard is full of thieves." He glanced at Nat's brown clothes. "Your pockets don't look worth picking, though."

14

Nat let that remark slide by. "What did the man look like?"

"Oh, lean and dark-haired. He moved like an eel."

A moment later, James Collier, Sir Dudley's secretary, turned into the alley. No mystery about that, Nat thought. Probably James Collier had a message for Andrew Downes and John Bois, two of the translators, who, along with Nat's father, were helping Sir Henry Savile with the St. Chrysostom book.

Collier, with pursed lips, passed the boys without a second glance, slippery as an eel.

"By the way, what are you doing here at Stationers' Hall?" the other boy asked.

"I'm on an errand. I have a message for my father."

"I'm on an errand, too. What's your father's name?"

"Dr. Nehemiah Culver."

"Oh, yes, one of the Bible translators, the newest on the list."

"How did you know that?" Nat demanded. "Are you the one making all the trouble for my father? Who are you, anyway?"

"Thomas Bushell, but call me Button. All my friends do. What are you called?"

Nat gave his nickname with reluctance. He could not keep down an uneasiness about Button. "How do you know about my father? Are you a spy for someone?"

Button laughed. "No, but I hear lots of gossip at court."

"At court?" Nat's interest quickened. "Are you a page to King James himself?" he asked in sudden awe.

Button fingered the twin row of buttons on his doublet. "You could say that." He hummed and rolled his eyes.

15

What an odd way of answering! Then Nat realized Button's suit was blue, not scarlet. Was Button lying? Nat remembered his mother's warning about being gullible. "Why aren't you wearing the King's colors?"

Button shrugged. "I can tell you're fresh from the country. You'd believe anything, wouldn't you?"

Nat winced. Mother had called it being gullible. "So you were lying."

"Not really. You just believed what you wanted to believe. Anyhow, if I did lie, it was worth it. You should have seen your eyes. They were as big as hen's eggs."

Nat grinned in spite of himself. It was hard to resist Button's high spirits, but he could not linger. He had to show Father the warning note. When Nat tried to enter Stationers' Hall the guard at the bottom of the entry steps would not let him in.

"I could have told you that," Button said. "You'll have to wait. Just like me. I know. I've been here before. I'm always running errands for my master."

"Who is he?"

"The adviser to King James."

Nat did not know whether to believe Button or not. Why would the King need an adviser? "What is his name?"

Button grinned, and Nat suspected there would be a mischievous answer. "Sir Hang Hog," Button said.

"I never heard of him."

"It's a joke," Button explained. "What's a hanged hog?"

That was easy to answer. Nat had lived in the country and knew about farm animals. "It's a pig."

"No, it's *bacon.*"

That was still no answer to Nat, but he saw that

16

Button relished the joke. It reminded him of Button's nickname. "Why are you called Button?"

"One of the buttons came loose on my new doublet and everyone at court started calling me Button."

The word *court* again caught Nat's attention. "How can you be at court and not work for King James?"

"You really are from the country," Button replied with scorn. "I work for the King's right-hand man, Mr. Francis Bacon." Button emphasized the *mister*.

"Is he one of the Bible translators?" Nat had met some of the translators, but there were six groups of them—two in London, two in Oxford (where Sir Henry Savile lived), and two in Cambridge. Nat had never heard the name Francis Bacon. *Mr.* Francis Bacon.

"He's not one of the six companies," Button said, "but who do you think made up the list of learned men in the first place?"

"King James." Everyone knew that. King James had ordered the revision of the Bible to be made, so he must have chosen the translators.

Button laughed aloud. "You certainly are an innocent. Don't you have any idea of how things are done at court?"

"King James sent out a proclamation." Nat was sure of what he was saying. Father had told the story many times—how the Puritans were not pleased with the translations in the Prayer Book, how they came to Hampton Court in 1604 and asked for a revision, how King James had said he had peppered the Puritans soundly, and that he did not want Jack and Tom and Will and Dick to censure him about this translation. "He wanted the names of the learned men of England," Nat told Button. "Bishops and people like that

17

sent him the names, and then he chose fifty-four to revise the Bible."

Button groaned in mock dismay. "Let me open your eyes a little. Someone had to check out the names. You don't think King James sat on his throne, looked over a list of names, and then decided which ones would revise the Bible, do you?"

Maybe not sat on his throne, Nat admitted to himself. Maybe he sat at a table. "But King James is a learned man, my father says. He studied the Bible when he was a child and even translated some of it from Latin, like the Book of Revelations and part of the Psalter."

"True, but King James likes hunting too much and giving parties and masques."

"What are masques?"

"Plays," Button explained. "One of the translators, Dr. Richard Edes, wrote plays. My master has written a lot of them. Not that he wants anyone to know. He even paid an actor to be the author of some of the long ones." For the first time, Button looked as if he had said too much. "Anyhow, my master is the King's right-hand man, at least for now. There's lots of gossip at court and gossip can change a lot of things overnight. But facts are facts. It was my master, the most learned man of all the learned men in England, who chose the translators."

Nat thought about what Button had said. Gossip could change things overnight. Had someone gossiped about Father's being at the bedside of Henry Percy in Paris? Was Father's name linked with the Gunpowder Plot? Had Francis Bacon heard the gossip and now wanted Father off the list of translators? *Was Francis Bacon Father's secret enemy?*

2

TOO MANY SPIES

While waiting with Button for permission to enter Stationers' Hall, Nat heard James Collier argue with the guard. "But I must see Sir Henry Savile immediately. I have an important message for him from his son-in-law, Sir Dudley Carleton."

"I am sorry," the guard said. "I cannot interrupt the translators. Your message will have to wait."

"But I must see him now. There has been a house search."

House search. Nat shuddered. When people were accused of being recusants or secret Catholics, their houses could be searched by the King's men without warning. If forbidden books were found, fines or imprisonment followed. But why would Sir Dudley Carleton's house be searched? Of what was he accused?

Before Nat could even try to answer the question the guard waved everyone inside. Button led the way to the open door of the translators' room. Nat saw the long table with large, open Bibles. He recognized the Geneva Bible, the one Father said King James thought the worst of all the previously translated Bibles.

A buzz of angry voices filled the room. Father's voice rose above the others.

"I am merely suggesting that we translate in the spirit and not just the word," he said.

The translators, all different in size and shape, stared at him. One translator had a long face and scraggly white hair. Another was short and stumpy, with small eyes. One little man hunched so low in his chair that his face almost touched the table. Large, ruddy-faced Andrew Downes frowned, laid his pen down, and leaned back in his chair.

"We must clear up this matter before we take our recess. Dr. Culver, we respect you as one of the ablest among us and have long wondered why you were not listed among the first rather than the last."

"The last shall be first," someone murmured.

"Now, Dr. Culver," Andrew Downes continued, "what is it that you think has been mistranslated in Luke 17:21?"

Father explained with his usual outspoken hearti-

Nat saw the long table with large, open Bibles. A buzz of angry voices filled the room.

ness. "The word should be *within*, not *among*. 'The kingdom of God is within you.' "

Another translator objected in an angry voice. "It should be *among*. The church—*ecclesia*—consists of people."

"The church is not something outside," Father replied. "It's inside, a spirit."

Some of the translators cleared their throats. Others shook their heads. Nat felt waves of hostility and realized Father's outspoken way had made more than one enemy. What would Father do when he saw the note? Was it one of the translators who wanted him out?

"We must confer with Lancelot Andrewes about the words *among* and *within*," someone suggested.

"He always says no true scholar will interrupt him before noon," another said with a smile.

"He may even joke about it," a third joined in. "Remember his play on words? 'If it be not Immanu-el, it will be Immanu-hell. But if we have Him, it will be Immanu-all."

"If we have the Dean of Westminster, we'll have to confer with the Dean of St. Paul's," the first translator said.

"Yes, if he's not too busy watching his wife."

To Nat's puzzlement, everyone smiled. Button whispered that John Overall, the dean, had a wife considered to be the most beautiful woman in England. Lancelot Andrewes, the Dean of Westminster, was a bachelor and did not have that problem. Button explained that Lancelot Andrewes and Francis Bacon were great friends. Both had touches of ill-health.

"We should also consult Dutch Thomson," someone said.

Several of the translators groaned. Was Dutch Thomson disliked? Button did not know the answer, but he did know about Dutch's nickname. "He came from the Low Countries," Button explained.

During the recess the translators walked up and down the hall talking. Nat tried to put the warning note into Father's hand, but James Collier brushed Nat aside. "Don't interrupt," he hissed. "There is important business going on."

Not only had there been a house search at Sir Dudley's but some of the St. Chrysostom notes had been taken into custody.

"But this is an outrage," Sir Henry roared. He called Andrew Downes, John Bois, and Father over to one side. These three men had been helping Sir Henry with the forthcoming book.

Button nudged Nat. "Mark my words, Sir Dudley's secretary is a spy."

"For whom?"

"There's talk at court that Sir Dudley was in the Gunpowder Plot. He was in Paris in 1603 with Henry Percy."

Nat gasped. Whatever had taken place in Paris was making trouble now. He felt an impulse to tell Button about Father being in Paris at that time, but something held him back. Better not add fuel to the fire of court gossip. Button would be sure to tell his master, Francis Bacon, anything he heard. It seemed to Nat that invisible enemies lurked on all sides. The facts could not be ignored. Someone had thrown a stone through the parish house window. Someone had written a note calling Father a traitor and warning him to withdraw.

Nat heard Sir Henry Savile give instructions to the

secretary, James Collier. "Get the other notes and bring them to Sir Dudley's." Sir Henry made his apologies to the others and left Stationers' Hall.

"What do you want?" Andrew Downes asked the secretary in a cold voice.

"The notes on St. Chrysostom, particularly John Bois's notes."

"Mine are better," Andrew Downes snapped. "After all, I was the teacher of John Bois."

"I am sorry if I have brought anyone grief," John Bois said. Smaller than Andrew Downes, John Bois was a quiet man with a certain hidden vigor about him, like one accustomed to daily walks. "Tell Sir Henry that my notes are safe," he told the secretary.

"But he wants to see them," James Collier said with a scowl.

"I have them stowed away."

"Shall I tell Sir Henry that?"

"I shall tell him." John Bois smiled, showing perfect teeth. "My notes are in my safe cabinet."

"And where is that?"

"My memory." John Bois smiled again.

"Is that the safest place?" the secretary asked.

"Yes, indeed. I am still chewing the cud."

John Bois's quiet manner seemed to soothe his teacher, Andrew Downes. The secretary went off, grumbling. Nat slipped the note into his father's hand, but before his father could read it, the translators were called back to continue their work. Nat heard Button give his message.

"My master wants to know when the Bible will be ready for the Privy Council."

"Why, tell him that we are still hammering," one of the translators said.

"We have taken the translations back to the anvil no fewer than fourteen times," another added.

"Closer to seventeen," someone else muttered.

Button had to leave without an answer. Nat went on home. Mother had gone to market and Nat started to work on his Hebrew lesson. A loud knock sounded on the front door. Nat sprang to his feet. A visitor already. Perhaps someone wanting to talk about the church program.

A messenger in royal red livery held up a sealed letter. The King's business, Nat thought. Perhaps a letter confirming Father as a translator for King James. When the messenger learned that Father was at Stationers' Hall, he insisted on going there with Nat. The guard immediately let him in and called Father out of the translators' room with two words, "King's business."

"What is this about?" he asked the messenger.

The messenger held up the sealed letter but did not hand it to Father.

"Let me get my spectacles and read it," Father said. He started back to the translators' room.

"Sir, you may not read it nor handle it. I am not to allow it to go out of my hands."

Nat noticed the messenger's hands were white and clean.

"Then how shall I know what it is?" Father asked.

"I have orders to read it to you, but I may not part with it."

"Does it concern the translating?"

The messenger hesitated. "In a manner of speaking, yes."

"Then let me take it home to my study where I have my books."

"In that case, I must go home with you into your study and sit with you until you have heard the message."

At home Father motioned Nat to come into the study, too.

"I do not want to be hasty with the King's business," Father said. "This will require time. I am not used to studying with someone sitting by me. I pray you leave the writing with me."

"No, sir. I am forbidden to leave it with you or to allow you to touch it."

Father paced the study. "How does this come about? I am no man's servant but the King's. I pray you tell His Majesty that I am dealt with neither manly nor scholar-like. If you have something to say in the King's name, I pray you, in plain terms, let me have it."

"You should withdraw," the messenger stated.

Father stopped and stared at the messenger. "You mean stop translating the Bible for King James? What is my fault that brings this about?"

"The King himself has so ordered."

"I know myself an honest man and therefore fear nothing," Father said. "I meddle with no man's quarrels. What causes the King to change toward me?"

"There are some things being buzzed around the court."

"What are they? Tell me, by all that is just and fair."

"You were in Paris in 1603."

"Yes, looking up manuscripts on St. Chrysostom for Sir Henry Savile, another of the translators for King James."

"That may be, but were you not at the bedside of the Earl of Northumberland when he lay ill?"

26

"Yes. I was called in to pray for him by Sir Dudley Carleton, who was not yet then Sir Henry's son-in-law."

"Know you not what admission you are making?"

"What admission am I making?" Father demanded. "Who can criticize a prayer for a sick man?" Father stated that he was not a Catholic sympathizer. "You mean I am accused of having something to do with the Gunpowder Plot? Why, you might as well accuse Sir Dudley Carleton of such a thing, or one of his servants. There was a manservant, James Collier, close by when I paid my one and only visit to the Earl. Why not accuse him?"

"I know nothing of that," the messenger said. "Let me read you the King's letter. 'Inasmuch as the King warrants it seemly at this time, because of divers remarks that cast opprobrium on the revising of his book, an early retirement from the company of revisers will be met with gracious acceptance.' "

"Then I must use the words of the psalmist," Father said. " 'He shall not be afraid of any evil tidings; for his heart standeth fast and believeth in the Lord.' "

"I have delivered the message." The messenger folded the letter, bowed and left. Father returned to Stationers' Hall.

Some time later another knock sounded at the door. Nat closed his Hebrew grammar book, dreading to find out what message there would be this time. When he opened the door he saw a workman in brown smock and thick shoes. The man held a hoe in one hand and three books in the other.

"Father isn't here," Nat told the man. "He's—"

The visitor interrupted, "I know, I know. He is with the other translators."

27

Perhaps the man might be wondering why Father was not attending church business, Nat thought. "The King is asking how soon the Bible will be ready for the printers," he told the workman.

"Never mind that." The man thrust the books into Nat's hands. "Your father did me a great favor. I have no money to pay him. Instead I make a gift of these books. They are my treasures." The man stroked the books with clean, white hands.

"I'm sure Father would not want me to accept them." In the country Father's parishioners had often brought gifts like chickens, vegetables, and fruits, but never books. Everyone knew Father was one of the learned men of England and they were in awe of him.

"I insist." With head ducked and shoulders hunched, the workman darted away.

Nat put the books on the table. There was something odd about this visitor. A workman in the common clothes of all workmen. But wait—his hands. Weren't they white—and clean? Strange, very strange. Nat remembered something else. He had forgotten to get the man's name. He had just taken the man's statements as truth. Gullible again! It was one thing to be good at Latin, Greek, and Hebrew, but why did he have to believe everything he heard?

Maybe the name was in the books the man had left. Nat leafed through them. No name. But the man had said they were his treasures. Why wouldn't he have put his name in them, then? Nat scanned the books more closely. He read about the Pope's wish for a Catholic England, how Catholics had a special dispensation to lie, if need be, to protect the priests who were making English converts to Catholicism.

Nat's head pounded with an upsurge of fear. These

books were illegal. To be caught with them would mean a fine, even imprisonment. He would have to get rid of them. Treasures, indeed. Why had the workmen left illegal books for Father?

Someone pounded on the rectory door. Nat groaned. What now? First, he would have to hide the books.

"Open up! Open up in the King's name."

There was no time to hide the books. With trembling hands Nat unbolted the door. Four soldiers in silver breastplates, plumed hats, and long pikes stormed inside.

"What do you want?" Nat could not keep the tremor from his voice.

"House search," the leader of the four soldiers snapped.

House search. Dreaded words. A forty-shilling fine for an unlawful book. One third of the fine to King James, one third to the finder, and one third for the poor of the parish.

Mother returned from marketing. "What can we do for you?" Her calm, polite tone comforted Nat. Mother could prevent the house search. The soldiers must not find the illegal books.

"We have been told recusants live here."

"But my husband is one of King James's Bible translators."

One of the soldiers picked up the illegal books and thumbed through them. "Look! Here are some of the forbidden books."

"Nat, where did those books come from?" Mother asked.

"A workman came in a little while ago and wanted Father to have them as a gift."

"What was the workman's name?"

29

"I don't know. I didn't ask." Nat felt Mother's glance. When would he learn not to take anything for granted? From now on he would not trust anyone. There were spies everywhere. Too many.

"These are Popish books," the leader of the soldiers declared. "Your husband is under arrest."

3

DANGEROUS MATTERS

The King's men seemed to know all about Father. They argued among themselves whether to go after him at Stationers' Hall or wait for him to come home.

"Go after him," one said. "March him through St. Paul's churchyard in disgrace. That will teach others a lesson."

"Let all disguised priests take warning," another said on the way out.

Mother whispered to Nat, "Find out what prison

they'll be taking your father to. It will be one of three—Clink, Fleet, or Newgate."

Nat followed the men to Stationers' Hall. Surely, the translators would see the injustice of Father's arrest and be able to stop it. Instead, Father came out of the building flanked by two of the King's men.

"Where are they taking him?" Nat asked the guard.

"Newgate prison."

Where could help be found? Not at Sir Dudley Carleton's. With a house search there and some of the St. Chrysostom notes in custody, fines and arrest might follow. Could Button help? His master, Francis Bacon was close to the King. *But can I believe what Button tells me?* Nat asked himself. Besides, Francis Bacon himself might be behind Father's arrest.

Nat trudged home. To his surprise Button was there.

"News spreads fast at court," he told Nat and Mother. "My master has heard about the arrest."

"You mean Father is now free?"

"Not at all." Button made a wry face. "The law doesn't work that fast, but my master thinks there is a plan afoot for some kind of Catholic uprising. He would like to see you."

"Now?" Nat headed for the door.

"Oh, no," Button laughed. Nat felt a familiar embarrassment. Would he ever learn how court affairs were handled? "Next week," Button told him.

During the days that followed, Nat and Mother visited Father at Newgate prison. Nat shrank from the stench of unclean, straw-covered floors, the clanging of metal bars, the shouts, curses, and moans of the prisoners. Father listened to his fellow prisoners and gave words of comfort to those without hope.

"There is a Catholic in here, too," he told Nat and Mother. "He's going to be executed soon. He faces his death with prayers of thanksgiving that he can die for the glory of God. Oh, that I could have such strength, such fortitude. If we had such men in the Church of England, there would be so much Christ consciousness that this country would be the herald of Christian faith."

To hear Father talk like that astounded Nat. Weren't Catholics to be hated? If they loved God that much, was it possible that God loved them, too?

The condemned priest discussed the new Bible translation with Father. "The English translation is heretical," the priest declared.

"Why?"

"It should be published only in the original languages—Hebrew, Greek, and Latin." He argued that the mistakes in translating from one language to another could distort God's Word.

Father admitted there had been some errors. Some of the translators wanted to use the word *elder* instead of *priest,* lest people think a Catholic priest was meant. "But in Hebrews 3:1 I insist we say 'High Priest of our profession, Christ Jesus.'"

The condemned priest approved, and on this friendly note said farewell. On the day of the execution Button persuaded Nat to go with him to Tyburn and watch. Hundreds of people jostled each other in their eagerness to watch a man die.

Nat felt sick to his stomach and pulled back. "I don't want to see anyone executed, even a Catholic."

Button shrugged and started off alone. "I'll go without you, then."

Nat found he could not go against the crowd. He

was borne along as if on a wave. At the scaffold many people fell to their knees asking the condemned man to bless them.

Moments before he was hanged, the priest told the crowd, "I am innocent of all charges except that of doing God's will." His courage never faltered.

When the terrible moment came, Nat gagged and tried to look away. A question he had never before thought of burned in his mind. *Wasn't Jesus crucified for doing God's will?*

After the execution Nat felt himself shoved, pushed back, stepped on, his cap knocked off, his coat ripped. People clawed their way to the dead man to get a relic, a bit of shoelace, or coat sleeve, or a drop of blood. How strange, Nat thought. By this priest's dying he had won the veneration of the spectators. Other priests would die, too. The traitors of the Gunpowder Plot were Catholics, but they had aroused the hatred of the people because they had tried to kill the King. Most of the secret Catholics wanted only to win converts, Nat was sure.

With Father in prison, Nat had to become an apprentice of some kind. Sir Henry Savile had a solution. His son-in-law, Sir Dudley Carleton, needed a page boy, and Nat's knowledge of Latin, Greek, and Hebrew would be of help in preparing the St. Chrysostom book.

On his first day at Sir Dudley's Nat found out from the servants that there had been no fines after the house search. "Sir Dudley has a most important protector at court," they whispered. "Salisbury." But the stolen Chrysostom papers—ah, that was another matter.

"Stolen?" Nat asked. "What can anyone do with them?"

"They are printed here sheet by sheet by John Norton, the printer, and the galley proofs are smuggled to Paris and sold," the servants said.

Nat noticed the servants kept out of the way of the secretary, James Collier. Nat soon found out why. The secretary was pulling out papers from various drawers and putting them in a wooden box with iron hinges.

"Don't go snooping around Sir Dudley's papers," he snarled.

"I'm just a page for Sir Dudley, that's all."

"Don't expect favors just because you have a friend at court."

"What friend?" All Nat could think of was Button, and he was not sure whether or not to consider Button a friend.

"I mean Sir Hang Hog," James Collier sneered. "Francis Bacon."

For the first time Nat understood the joke Button had made about Francis Bacon's name.

James Collier was not through with his warnings. "I understand you are to be a favorite around here. If I ever catch you among Sir Dudley's papers, I'll thrash you, and if you ever tell on me, I'll thrash you doubly."

Startled, shocked, outraged, Nat managed to keep silent. Tell? What would there be to tell? A fanatical gleam in James Collier's eyes aroused Nat's wonder. He had not seen an expression that tense since the execution of the Catholic priest.

Nat kept out of James Collier's way. He learned what pages do—fetching books, paper, or pen and ink for Sir Dudley, and running errands. By evening he was so tired he slumped on a little stool near the front door and dozed. When would Sir Dudley dismiss him for the night? Nat longed to go to bed in the little room assigned to him at the foot of the stairway. The other servants retired one by one.

Someone tapped on the door. Nat sprang up, alert. His master must be expecting a late visitor. But how strange. At this hour of the night?

He unlatched the door. A man pushed his way in.

"Is this the 'ome of Sir Dudley Carleton?"

Nat resented the man's arrogant tone. "Yes, sir."

" 'e's expecting me, in a manner of speaking."

The man reminded Nat of someone, but he could not figure out who.

"What name shall I give, sir?"

"Never mind the name. Just say I'm from court."

Nat was puzzled. The man's velvet cap was dirty, the cape flung over one shoulder was threadbare, and the laces on his pointed shoes broken and tied. Sir Dudley would certainly not want to see a man like that.

"There's someone at the door asking for you, sir," Nat told Sir Dudley.

"At this hour of the night? Who is it?"

"He won't give his name, sir. He says he is from court."

Sir Dudley hummed under his breath. "I hope it isn't someone offering me Irish employment. I would have to decline. It doesn't pay enough, and if I am offered employment at Venice or the Low Countries again, I shall decline them also. But enough of that. We shall have to see what the courtier wants. Send him in."

The visitor eased his way in to Sir Dudley's workroom and stood with cap in hand.

"And what may I do for you?" Sir Dudley asked, motioning Nat to stay behind his chair.

"It isn't for me—it's for you."

There was something familiar about the man. Where had Nat seen him before? Was it at St. Paul's churchyard, perhaps? There was something about the man's stocky build that nudged at Nat's memory.

"You remember the Earl?"

Sir Dudley straightened and leaned forward. "Indeed I do. Everyone at court knows that I was at the Earl's side in Paris, that he and I did not agree, that I was ordered home and was confined in the bailiff's house here in Westminster for a time."

The visitor fumbled with his cap. "You knew he was connected with the Gunpowder Plot."

"Yes, yes, of course. I left his employ years ago, as everyone knows."

"Lately there has been gossip at court, sir, that says you know more about the Plot than you have let on, but with your help I can arrange to have such talk denied."

Sir Dudley leaned back in his chair. "What you are trying to say, you scoundrel, is that you want me to pay you to protect my good name."

The man lifted one hand in protest. His clean white hands contrasted to his worn clothes in a way that puzzled Nat. "No, sir," the man said. "I just came to warn you that there'll be something made of this talk, what with the Catholics plotting to take over the country. I'm just saying that you'd better watch what you say and what you write. Just a friendly warning, sir, that's all I had in mind. Of course, if you had a sovereign to spare to aid me get back to my poor sick mother in Ireland, it would be a godsend, but that's entirely up to you, sir. I came here of my own free will, as a service."

Sir Dudley gave the man a coin. "It's only for your poor sick mother that I'm doing this."

"I understand, sir, and God bless you and protect you from the evil talk at court."

With a fleeting glance at Nat, the man left. That glance shook Nat like a strong wind. This man was the same workman in brown smock who had left the illegal books causing Father's arrest. But how could this be? All the tiredness left Nat. He itched to question the man. Was he the link to the mystery about Father?

Sir Dudley sat with his hands on his forehead. "The Gunpowder Plot again. I am innocent and can prove it again if need be. A Catholic uprising, he said, that visitor of ours. I can almost believe it. Just last April old Lady Montague died in Sussex. She kept a chapel and pulpit, heard Mass, housed many Catholics, and even had a house by the Thames near the bridge to hide priests coming into England." He stood up. "But why am I remembering that when there is important business at hand. Nat, I want you to follow that man. See where he lives, what he does, the people he talks to."

Too late already, Nat thought, but he darted out to the hall. The courtier-like man was talking to James Collier. Not talking. Arguing was more like it. Was he trying to get money from James Collier, too?

"I have done many services for you," the man was saying. "I need the money now. Why don't you pay me what you owe?"

"I'll pay, I'll pay," James Collier growled. "Meet me at St. Paul's tomorrow, same time as always."

"I can't. I have to rehearse for a masque at court tomorrow night."

So the man was an actor! Nat slipped behind the stairwell and tried to digest this bit of information. One point was clear. This actor must have thrown the stone through the parish house window after bribing the children in the neighborhood either to keep silent or make a nuisance of themselves exploding gunpowder. But the actor would not have written the note. The man who hired him wrote the note—James Collier, secretary to Sir Dudley Carleton. Why? The question lingered in Nat's mind. He huddled in the dark corner of the stairwell and listened to the rise and fall of the two men's voices. The actor wanted his money. James Collier was not going to pay it then.

"I tell you I haven't got it now. Remember, you are part of a great work, and the time will come when you will be paid well for all your pains."

Nat heard the door close. He peered out. Neither James Collier nor the actor was in sight. He let himself out into the cold night air and listened for footsteps. Had the two men gone somewhere together? All the houses were dark. The silence pressed around him. There was no way for him to follow anyone when he could not even hear footsteps.

A sudden thought came to Nat. James Collier had been putting papers in a wooden box. What were those papers? Could they possibly be the St. Chrysostom notes? The ones James Collier had said were taken in custody after the house search? Was Sir Dudley's secretary stealing them, having them published, sending them to Paris, selling them?

The idea excited Nat. He would tell Sir Dudley about the actor, wait his chance next day when James

Collier had gone out, and explore the papers in the wooden box. Maybe the whole mystery could be cleared up.

The next day Nat did not have a moment to himself. Besides, there were too many people bustling about the house. Servants and visitors moved in and out. Sir Henry came, upset over the missing notes, yet still helping with the Bible translations at Stationers' Hall.

"We're doing all we can about your father," he told Nat. "He is permitted to work on the St. Chrysostom notes, and we hope to have him back soon on the final draft of the Bible. As soon as he is cleared of charges, of course."

That night Nat waited until the servants went to bed. James Collier left the house on some mysterious errand of his own, and Nat found the wooden box covered with a velvet cloth. He did not dare put it on the table but knelt by it with a candle that cast weird shadows on the wall. The box was locked. Where was the key? Nat groaned in dismay. Would he have to search all night?

He heard a slight sound and looked up. A shadow darker than the others loomed over him.

"So I've caught you spying on me!" James Collier grabbed Nat's shoulder. "You thought I had gone out, didn't you? But I knew what was on your mind all day." He jerked Nat to his feet. "I'm going to give you that double thrashing I promised to make sure you will tell no one about what you have done."

Nat clenched his hands and braced himself for the first blow.

"So I've caught you spying on me!" James Collier grabbed Nat's shoulder. "You thought I had gone out, didn't you?"

4

THE HIGH AND THE LOW

The next minute Nat heard Sir Dudley call out from the upper hall. "What is going on down there?"

At the sound of Sir Dudley's voice, James Collier changed instantly. He let go of Nat and became a quiet servant.

"To bed, to bed, both of you," Sir Dudley ordered.

"Yes, sir." James Collier bowed in the direction of Sir Dudley but hissed in an aside to Nat, "I won't forget this." He took the box with him.

That box! Nat was sure it contained the answer to all that had happened. He longed to open it somehow, pry it open if necessary. Unable to sleep in his narrow bed under the stairs, Nat asked the questions that had to be answered. Why was James Collier paying an actor to stir up trouble? The stone-throwing incident, although no one had seen that. The illegal books that caused Father's arrest. Before that, the King's messenger. That was not someone sent by the King. *The messenger was the actor, too.* The sudden realization made Nat sit up in bed. All these things were connected. But why? What was James Collier trying to achieve? Was he stealing some of the St. Chrysostom papers, having them printed, and sending them to Paris to be sold? If so, what did he do with the money?

In the next few days Nat saw that Sir Henry Savile trusted James Collier. They worked at a big table piled with papers and books. Even though Sir Henry belonged to the Oxford second company of translators, on his London visits he divided his time between Stationers' Hall and his son-in-law's. "The work of translating the Bible still goes forward," he told Sir Dudley. "The Old Testament is done." He sighed. "We need Richard Thomson. He's a master of word roots."

"Is he—uh—ill?" Sir Dudley asked.

"He won't answer his door."

Nat saw a quick glance exchanged between Sir Henry and Sir Dudley.

"Perhaps a new voice would persuade him to come to Stationers' Hall." Sir Henry glanced at Nat.

"Is he the one called *Dutch?*" Nat asked.

Sir Henry nodded and explained how to find Dutch's house. A little later, Nat knocked on Dutch Thomson's door. After a moment someone shuffled to the door and opened it a crack. Nat glimpsed a man with a high, white forehead and a red nose.

"Who is it?" The man's voice sounded muffled.

"Nathaniel Culver, sir."

"Do I know you?"

"No, sir."

"Who sent you?"

Nat thought fast. If he said Sir Henry Savile, Dutch Thomson might refuse to let him in. "Sir Dudley Carleton," he said.

The man slurred the name in bitter tones. "Why, he's an important man at King James's court. Not as close as Francis Bacon, of course. What business does Sir Dudley have with me?"

Nat started to explain but caught himself. A sudden doubt sprang into his mind. Was he talking to the right man? "Are you Richard Thomson?"

The man chuckled. "No."

"Oh, excuse me, sir. I'll leave." But it was the right house. Nat had made sure of it.

"Don't go, don't go. Just my little joke. Everyone calls me Dutch. Come in."

Nat followed Dutch Thomson through an entrance hall to an inner room. On a long table, like others Nat had seen, lay several open Bibles and papers pushed almost to the edge. Dutch Thomson sank into a chair and sat for a moment with both hands pressed to His forehead. There was a a peculiar vinegary smell throughout the book-lined room.

"I can't seem to collect my wits this morning," Dutch Thomson said. "Now, what is this about Sir Dudley what-is-his-name?"

Only the truth would do, Nat decided. "His father-in-law is Sir Henry Savile."

Dutch frowned as if the name meant nothing.

"One of the Bible translators."

With a laugh that was half groan, Dutch Thomson nodded several times. "Of course, of course. We translators had better call ourselves revisers of the Bible. The new version will be a hodgepodge."

Nat's curiosity was aroused. "Why do you say that?"

"There's already the treacle Bible," Dutch said.

"What kind of Bible is that?"

Dutch thumbed through one of the open Bibles. "Right here in Coverdale's Bible of 1535 it says in Jeremiah 8:22, 'There is no more treacle in Gilead.' Treacle is molasses. What a ridiculous translation. It's in the Bishops' Bible of 1568, too. I wonder what translation King James's revisers will make?" Dutch Thomson picked up a Geneva Bible of 1560. "Of course, we could still use the 'breeches' Bible, but King James doesn't like it."

"Why was it called that?" Nat asked.

Dutch Thomson read Genesis 3:7. " 'And they sewed figtree leaves together and made themselves breeches.' Before that, we had the 'bugs' Bible." He read Psalm 91:5 in Matthews Bible of 1551. " 'Thou shalt not need to be afraid for any bugs by night.' "

Nat almost forgot his errand. The problems of translating puzzled him. If people made mistakes, how could they be sure God's Word was coming through?

"I am sure you were not sent here to listen to me talk about translating," Dutch Thomson said.

"No, sir. Shouldn't we be going?"

Dutch bristled. "Going where?"

"To Stationers' Hall."

"Whatever for? I'm doing my work here." He slouched in his chair. "To tell the truth, I agree with

45

Hugh Broughton. He was not among the chosen because of his bad temper. He would not allow any scholar in the world to cross him in Hebrew and Greek when he was sure he had the truth." Dutch quoted Dr. Broughton's exaggerated dismay at the Bishops' Bible. " 'The cockles of the sea shores and the leaves of the forest, and the grains of the poppy, may as well be numbered as the gross errors of this Bible.' "

Nat saw that Dutch Thomson had no intention of leaving the house. In fact Dutch became annoyed at the idea. "Why would Sir Dudley send his page boy to me when Sir Dudley has nothing to do with revising the Bible? Answer me that, Nathaniel whatever-your-name-is."

Nat understood the hidden message behind Dutch Thomson's teasing words: Dutch would not be going to Stationers' Hall. Nevertheless, he answered the question by explaining that Sir Henry discussed the translations with his son-in-law, and besides, Sir Dudley was helping with the St. Chrysostom editing.

Dutch Thomson shook his head several times, each time slower than the last. "It's too much. By doing both, how can he be fair to either one? Translating—I mean revising—the Bible is enough for any scholar. There are many decisions to make."

"You mean whether or not to use a word like *bugs?*" Nat asked, interested in spite of feeling more and more uncomfortable.

Dutch Thomson nodded and kept on nodding. "Very important. But they have to decide what books to use."

"Books? You mean to help them translate?"

"No, I mean the books to be included in the Bible."

Nat was mystified. He had heard the phrase *books of the Bible* but never understood before that such

46

books could be included or omitted. Didn't the Bible come from God? Who would dare omit any of His books? "But isn't the Bible one book?" he asked in spite of his new understanding.

"No. The Bible is many books." Dutch Thomson suddenly slapped the table with his open hand. "I say we should include the thirty-three books omitted by the Council of Nicaea in 307. No one else agrees with me. No one." He reached for a carafe of wine and poured himself a glass.

"Oh, please, sir, shouldn't we be going?"

"Going where?"

"To Stationers' Hall, where the others are."

"Ah, yes, the others. There's the Dean of Westminster. Angel in the pulpit. That's Lancelot Andrewes. Understands fifteen languages. Keeps Christmas all year. Has a private chapel. Popish, I call it, with its altar, candlesticks, gilt canister for wafers, cushions, and I don't know what all. Yet he preaches recusants right back into the Church of England. Yes, the Dean is an important person. More important than I'll ever be." Dutch Thomson refilled his glass.

"That is not true, sir. You are one of the learned men of England. That's why you were chosen to help with the King's book."

Dutch Thomson nodded again and again. Nat wished he would stop.

"Then you'll come?" he asked.

Dutch slammed the glass down. "Don't they know I'm ill," he shouted. He buried his face in his hands. "I'm ill," he mumbled.

Of course. That was why Dutch Thomson was acting in such a strange way.

"I'll tell them that you're ill, sir."

Dutch Thomson lifted his head, his eyes red-rimmed and bloodshot. "I'm not ill. I'm never ill. Who said I was? Was it the Dean of St. Paul, that overall Latinist, John Overall? He has spoken Latin so long it bothers him to speak English." Dutch brooded a moment. "Maybe it was that country preacher, John Bois. No gentleman, he. His family didn't own a clod of dirt. His father was only a cloth maker from Halifax."

Nat remembered John Bois' quiet manner. "I don't think he would ever say anything like that."

"What do you know about it?" Dutch Thomson growled.

"My father is one of the translators, but—" Nat found himself telling the whole story to a drunken man. It was so plain to Nat now. Why hadn't he realized it before? The answer was simple. He had not expected a man in such a high position to be so low. How could God's Word be correctly translated by someone who was not sober? Why was an innocent man like Father in jail?

"So your father is Dr. Culver." Dutch Thomson gathered up papers and put them in a large leather pouch. "He's in jail and I'm not. The work must go forward." He motioned Nat to the door.

Was he going, or was he going to give the translations to Nat to take to Stationers' Hall?

"I'll carry it for you, sir."

"No, you won't, Nathaniel Culver. My translations stay with me."

Near St. Paul's churchyard, Dutch Thomson told Nat to go on ahead and tell the translators that he was coming.

"Oh, sir, I'd better stay with you."

Dutch Thomson clutched the leather bag closer. "I

am perfectly all right. I insist that you go on ahead."

Nat started off, but looked over his shoulder several times. At Stationers' Hall Nat waited for a recess, feeling a little foolish giving Dutch Thomson's message. After all, Dutch would be there before Nat had time to tell anyone.

Andrew Downes heard the message. His long, ruddy face reddened even more in exasperation, and his lively eyes glowed with impatience. "Can't Richard Thomson ever get any place on time? When I think of the time and trouble I take coming to London from Cambridge, I'm ready to give up translating altogether, to say nothing of my work on St. Chrysostom." He glared at John Bois. "Your work seems to be favored by Sir Henry, but mark my words, the money you earn will burn in your pocket."

After a few minutes the translators went back to their work. Dutch Thomson had not appeared. Nat went back to St. Paul's churchyard. A group of people surrounded someone lying on the cobblestones. Nat pushed his way through. Dutch Thomson lay sprawled, one arm over a pile of papers strewn from an open leather bag.

A housewife stood with her hand to her mouth. "Oh, pray help the poor man. He's ill."

"His face is so red. He must have a fever," another said.

The onlookers stirred and murmured, but no one moved to help.

Nat did not know what to do. He had never seen a man dead drunk. But the Bible translations—they had to be saved. Nat knelt and gathered them up. His action prompted others to lift Dutch Thomson to a sitting position.

Someone choked out the dreaded words, "It's the sickness."

"The sickness!" People drew back in horror, letting Dutch Thomson slump down. They scrambled over each other in their haste to escape. Nat knew what was meant. The ever-present plague snuffed out lives. Chills, fever, delirium, inflammations brought about a horrible death without respect to high or low.

Nat fought the impulse to run, even though he knew Dutch Thomson did not have 'the sickness.' Yet how could he be sure? Maybe Dutch Thomson was not only drunk but had the plague as well. Hadn't Mother said not to take anything for granted? Nat made a firm decision. He was not going to leave Dutch Thomson. He would take care of the papers.

Two men in long robes came toward him, Lancelot Andrewes and John Overall. They did not seem surprised to see Dutch Thomson.

The onlookers at a safe distance cried out in excitement, "It's the Dean of Westminster!"

"And the Dean of St. Paul's."

The two men assured the crowd that it was not the plague and had servants take Dutch Thomson home. Nat returned to Sir Dudley's house. Neither Sir Dudley nor James Collier was there.

"As soon as the master left, Collier left, too," Nat was told. "Another of his mysterious errands."

The box! Now was his chance. Nat determined to hunt through the whole house for the box if he had to. The key would be a different matter. Should he pry the box open when he found it?

But there was no problem. The box lay on the study table, with the key in the lock. It was too good to be true. Nat made sure no servants were around and opened the box. Empty. He should have known. James Collier must have set this up as a trap.

At the sound of voices in the front hall, Nat scurried back to the servants' quarters. In a few minutes he heard Sir Dudley calling for him in the study. It couldn't be about the box, Nat told himself. He had not done anything wrong, except snoop a little.

James Collier was with Sir Dudley. "I tell you, sir, that boy has been in your papers, though I warned him not to do it."

"Is that true, Nat?"

How did James Collier know? Nat took a deep breath. "I opened the box."

"You see?" James Collier's triumphant expression worried Nat. Why was an empty box so important?

The next question shook Nat to his toes.

"Where are the papers that were in that box?" James Collier asked.

"It was empty," Nat faltered. He sensed what James Collier was trying to do.

"Some more of the St. Chrysostom papers have been stolen," Sir Dudley said. "They are very valuable. Sir Henry is spending his fortune to have them published."

"I know, sir, but I know nothing about them."

The secretary left the room, came back and beckoned Sir Dudley. Nat followed. To his horror, he saw James Collier go to the little bed under the stairs, lift the coverlet, and bring out a pile of papers.

Speechless, Nat stared at James Collier and glimpsed a smirk of triumph on the secretary's face. *How low the mighty have fallen,* Collier's expression seemed to say. *Sir Dudley won't think so highly of you now.*

5

A NEW START

The leather bag containing Dutch Thomson's Bible translations lay on top of Nat's bed. He handed it to Sir Dudley, hoping that somehow the loose papers James Collier had found were Bible translations and not the missing St. Chrysostom papers. But that hope failed. The facts were plain. The St. Chrysostom papers had been found on Nat's bed and he could not explain how they got there.

When Sir Henry Savile arrived later with Andrew

Downes and John Bois, Nat heard Sir Henry tell them how much it would cost to have the St. Chrysostom book printed. "It is two thousand pounds for the paper alone," he said. Special type had been brought from Holland for the book. Sir Henry was giving his entire fortune for the publication.

Nat remembered that Sir Henry's only son would have been Nat's age. If the son had lived, Sir Henry would not have undertaken the task of furthering knowledge by the printing of St. Chrysostom's writings. Now he had to worry about theft.

Expecting James Collier to accuse him openly, Nat was surprised to hear himself praised.

"I recommend this young scholar for his good wit," James Collier told Sir Henry.

"A plague on him," Sir Henry exploded. "Give me the plodding student. If I would look for wits I would go to Newgate prison. There be the wits."

Newgate prison! Nat had not thought ahead that far. Father, who was innocent, was there. *Will they send me there, too?* To his surprise, no one called him a thief. In fact the discovery of the St. Chrysostom papers on his bed was not mentioned by Sir Dudley. Why didn't James Collier make an accusation? Why had he praised Nat? Was he sorry for what he had done? Nat could not believe that. There must be some other scheme James Collier had in mind.

The men talked about secret Catholics in England, how the pope a few years before allowed them to deny being Catholics.

"The Gunpowder plotters would have been sainted at Rome," Andrew Downes said.

Sir Henry Savile mentioned that Dr. John Reynolds, a Bible translator at Oxford who had died many months before, had first been a Papist. "His brother William was a Protestant. Then Dr. Reynolds became a Protestant and his brother a Papist."

Sir Dudley mentioned in his turn the court gossip about Lady Mary Lovell and Lord Vaux's mother being suspected of harboring disguised priests in their homes. "The King is determined to revive the 'King's silver' poll tax. It is to be paid on taking the yearly oath of allegiance as a safeguard against popery," Sir Dudley said. "The profits are to be used to erect a college at Chelsea for the better handling of religious controversies."

The men agreed that even the new translation of the Bible would not stop controversies. As for a special college where controversies could be smoothed out, Sir Dudley thought Francis Dillingham, one of the Bible translators of the first Cambridge group, could be of help.

"He wrote about the golden key to eternal happiness," Andrew Downes said, "but I don't think he would be of much help when people disagree. He's always quoting from the Geneva Bible, even though he knows King James detests it."

Sir Dudley brought up the name of Laurence Chaderton, a Puritan, also in the first Cambridge group. Chaderton's father was for the pope and disinherited his son.

"I know of forty men who are now clergymen because of Laurence Chaderton's preaching," Andrew Downes admitted. He marveled that Chaderton was over seventy years old and had never required eyeglasses.

Nat listened to the men plan their imaginary college with various Bible translators as teachers. There was

John Richardson, called fat and dull by Andrew Downes, yet good in public dispute, and an excellent Hebraist. Thomas Ravis had died recently and had been quietly buried. He had been more than a translator and preacher. He had brought water by conduits to important houses near Gloucester.

"But he would never do in the college the King wants to set up," Sir Henry said. "Ravis had vowed that no preacher in his district would remain there if he did not conform."

"It amounted to persecution," John Bois murmured.

Among other names, Richard Thomson's was brought up. "Lancelot Andrewes thinks the world of him, but a drunk man argues too much," Sir Henry said. "Certainly Hugh Broughton would never do at that college. His terrible temper kept him off the list of translators."

Roger Andrewes might have a place in the college, although he was less distinguished than his brother Lancelot. George Abbott, on the other hand, might not fit in. "Did you know he has West Indian sapphires, gold and silver bracelets, and even a gold basin?" Sir Dudley asked. "Not that it matters, but he's quite choleric and that makes him quarrelsome."

William Barlow, whose sermons had pleased Queen Elizabeth, was considered unfair by the Puritans.

Why didn't the men talk about more important matters than an imaginary college? Nat asked himself. Like Father's imprisonment. Like the St. Chrysostom papers found in Nat's bed. He was convinced James Collier had put them there. But why? What had Collier hoped for?

The questions buzzed through Nat's head like the drone of the men's voices. He went outside and stood in the moonlight near the door, out of earshot of Sir Dudley and the others. He heard the gate of the back garden open cautiously and ducked behind a bush just in time to see James Collier glide past. What secret errand was he on? It would be easy to follow him at a safe distance.

Nat darted from one house to the next, keeping James Collier in sight. James Collier stopped at a big house, a nobleman's house, Nat was sure. Collier greeted people who came up one by one, all muffled to the ears by their hats and cloaks. They entered the house without knocking.

With a sudden burst of understanding, Nat knew the people were secret Catholics, illegally meeting for a religious service, and James Collier was one of them. But how could it be proved? The answer was simple. Nat could not prove anything. If he spied on them, he would be caught. Nothing would be gained. "I can't tell anyone about this," Nat told himself. Not after the St. Chrysostom episode.

Back at Sir Dudley's Nat heard the men still talking. He slumped on the little stool by the door and was relieved when he heard someone knock. Somehow he was not surprised to open the door and see the actor. Maybe this time Nat could find out more about James Collier, maybe even proof that Collier was a Catholic.

"Is James Collier in?" the actor asked.

"No, he went out. May I take a message?"

A spasm crossed the actor's face. "Where did he go? I must find him."

For a second, Nat hesitated. Should he take the risk? "I can show you where he went." There. He had said it.

"Please do. Thank you very much."

In front of the nobleman's house Nat stopped the actor and motioned to him to listen. From inside came the faint sounds of chanting in Latin.

The actor clutched Nat's arm. "But that is popish."

"Yes. James Collier is a secret Catholic," Nat said matter-of-factly.

The actor shuddered. "A Catholic! He can't be! He told me this was to save England from traitors. He said I would be doing a great service to the King. He said he'd pay me well, but he hasn't paid me at all."

"Where was he going to get the money?" Nat well knew that James Collier's wages were no higher than those paid other servants.

"From a sale of valuable manuscripts that had been willed to him," the actor explained. "I don't want anything to do with Catholics, though. I can't afford fines or imprisonment."

"What can be done?" Nat asked.

"Does Sir Dudley know James Collier is a Catholic?" the actor asked.

"No."

"Then tell him," the actor urged.

"I can't."

"Why not?"

"I have no proof."

The actor laughed. "That's easy. Just leave some popish books in his clothes chest at the foot of his bed or under his bed covers."

Nat explained why he could not do that. "I've been caught once, and besides, he put those St. Chrysostom papers under my bed covers. Sir Dudley hasn't told me yet what is going to happen because of it."

The actor brooded a moment. "I could come in one of my disguises—"

"Like a workman?"

"Yes, yes, that would do." The actor hunched over like a work-weary laborer. "I play that part well."

Nat could not resist a spirit of mischief. "You could leave some illegal books with the servants and tell them the books are gifts for a favor Sir Dudley had done for you."

"Yes, I've done that before. That's what James Collier hired me to do with a certain Dr. Culver."

The mischief Nat had felt turned into an instant rage. "He is my father."

"Your father?"

"Yes, and he was arrested and put in Newgate prison."

"Well, he is innocent," the actor said.

"Then you can free him by telling the truth."

The actor groaned. "I can't do that. It would connect me with James Collier. It would ruin me. I wish I had never hired out to him, but I needed the money. My mother is ill."

Was this acting? Nat could not be sure. "Your mother is in Ireland, isn't she?"

"Yes, yes. How did you know?"

"I was there when you came to warn Sir Dudley about the court gossip."

"Ah, one of my better disguises. I thought I handled that rather well. If only James Collier had paid me. Now, if he did pay me, I would not dare take it. I cannot take chances with my good name at court."

"Then you won't help my father?"

"I'm afraid not. But I'll do this. I'll drop a word, so to speak, after tomorrow's masque to Francis Bacon. He wrote it, and he's a lawyer, King James's right-hand man at the moment. Bacon is very modest about his plays, but all the actors like to play the parts he writes." The actor sighed. "But I've had my fill of this part I've played with James Collier. Strange that I could not see he was acting a part. I trust that justice will be done."

After the actor left, Nat tiptoed to the room where the three Bible translators and Sir Dudley were still talking, this time about the King's book. Nat had heard the words many times and had thought they meant the Bible. To his astonishment, he learned that the King's book of instructions was covered in velvet, with coats of arms, corner pieces in gold, and stamped with a rose, thistle, lion, and lilies. It had a silk ribbon dangling at each corner. In the book King James disagreed with the Pope's instructions to Catholics in England not to take the Oath of Allegiance.

Nat decided that for him the King's book would always be the Bible the translators were now working on.

"Will there be a preface to our Bible?" John Bois asked.

"If so, not like Whittingham's preface to the Geneva Bible," Andrew Downes snapped. "You know, where he talks about three classes of men, the third sort being simple lambs, partly already in the fold of Christ and partly wandering astray by ignorance."

"But he does say the Shepherd will find them," Sir Henry said.

"I heard a Catholic say stained-glass windows in churches are the poor man's Bible," Sir Dudley remarked. "Therefore, it is not necessary that Catholics should have or read a Bible in their mother tongue."

"Wycliffe fought that battle long ago, and won it, in spite of his bones being dug up and burned at the command of the Pope," Sir Henry said, "His Bible and Tyndale's give us the roots of English. As for a preface to King James's Bible, I cannot say whether or not there should be one. We might be like Cranmer in the Bishops' Bible when he said he hoped it would be sold and read by every person until such time that the bishops should set forth a better translation, and that, in his opinion, would not be until a day after doomsday."

The talking came to an end without any decision being made about a preface to the new Bible. The men left the house, agreeing to come back the next day for further work on the St. Chrysostom book. James Collier slipped in and quietly went to his room. Sir Dudley went upstairs, and Nat found himself alone. Nothing had been said about whether he was considered to be a thief or whether he was not. Puzzled, he went to bed under the stairs wondering if he had been living a dream.

The next morning James Collier must have read Nat's face.

"Don't think Master has forgotten," he growled.

"Why don't you have me arrested?" Nat asked boldly.

"Your time will come."

Nat could not help but wonder. He had a wild idea of going to Francis Bacon and pleading his case. But what good would that do? He had no proof of any of the things he knew about. He could not follow James Collier around all day. The big question was always there. Why was James Collier doing all these things? Why had he gone to so much trouble to have Father imprisoned? Just being a secret Catholic did not explain what Nat needed to know.

All day long, James Collier kept glancing at Nat with an air of something about to happen. Sir Dudley kept busy as always, writing to his friend John Chamberlain, reading, going over papers, giving orders to servants. All the time, Nat felt something building up.

Late in the afternoon, James Collier left the house. John Bois arrived first from Stationers' Hall. Sir Dudley greeted him, and Nat heard the murmur of their voices.

"Nat, would you come here, please," Sir Dudley requested.

It was coming, whatever it was going to be. Nat stood at the head of the big table, looking at John Bois, who sat across from Sir Dudley. Nat had time to wonder why Sir Dudley called him in after James Collier had left the house. Why wasn't Collier there ready to accuse him of theft?

"As you know, Nat, there has been some trouble about the St. Chrysostom papers."

I didn't take them, Nat wanted to cry out, but he realized he was not hearing any accusation in Sir Dudley's words.

"Something has to be done, of course, and I think we have the perfect solution." Sir Dudley nodded toward John Bois.

"I need a tutor for my six-year-old son," John Bois said in his mild voice.

Nat sighed. He had not been accused of theft. Not only that, he had been offered another position.

"You can take post horses to Cambridge," John Bois explained. "Then walk the five miles across the fields." Mrs. Bois and the four children lived at Boxworth.

"It will be a new start for you," Sir Dudley said.

Nat agreed and smiled his thanks.

6

LOOSE ENDS

How could he leave London with Father still in jail, and the mystery of his imprisonment unsolved? And what about the visit with Francis Bacon? Nat had expected Button to come and tell him when he was to go. He still burned with embarrassment at how Button had laughed at Nat's ignorance of the way things were handled at court. Besides, would it do any good to see Mr. Bacon? Would he listen to what Nat could tell about James Collier? Without proof?

With these thoughts running through his mind, Nat forgot to ask when he would have to leave London for Cambridge and Boxworth. By the time the question occurred to him, Sir Henry and Andrew Downes arrived discussing one of the Bible translation problems. What would be the final translation of 1 Samuel 10:24? Coverdale's 1535 Bible said, "God save the new king."

"Coverdale's Bible was put forth in hot haste," Andrew Downes complained.

In Matthew's Bible of 1537 and the Great Bible put out in 1539 by Whitchurch, the printer, the passage read, "God lend the king life."

English exiles had put out a Bible in Geneva in 1560. It and the Bishops' Bible of 1568 said, "God save the king."

"I wonder why the King does not like the Geneva Bible," Sir Dudley said. "It has the best paper, silver type, and is the first Bible to be in verses, easy to read."

"Its notes are a deadweight," Sir Henry told him.

"Scripture should stand alone," John Bois agreed.

While the men were talking, James Collier returned. Nat ducked out of sight and later told the servants that he would be leaving.

"No matter what Collier tells us, we know you are not a thief," they assured Nat. "But Collier steals out by owl-light. Where does he go?"

Nat did not answer. He had no proof. If he told what he had seen and heard, it would just make gossip.

The next morning in his tiny room under the stairs, Nat bundled up his clothes. Sir Dudley gave him money for post horses. Nat understood without a word being spoken that John Bois had little money. The translators were not paid. Some were already rich, like Sir Henry Savile. Others were paid in food and lodging when they worked at Oxford or Cambridge. Of course, when the St. Chrysostom book was finished, Sir Henry would pay Andrew Downes, John Bois, and Father well for their work.

Father. Nat had almost forgotten. Before he left London he would ask Father to recall every detail of his trip to Paris in 1603. Father had the missing key to the mystery, whether or not he knew it.

"Did you see James Collier in Paris?" Nat asked on his visit to Newgate prison.

"One time a strange incident happened," Father remembered. "James Collier was carrying a box and going upstairs ahead of me to the Earl's apartment. Collier went into an antechamber and disappeared."

"Disappeared?" Nat asked.

"Yes. When I came from the Earl's bedside, there was no one in the antechamber except a Catholic priest. His back was turned to me. Naturally, I didn't want to have anything to do with a priest, so I didn't speak to him, but I wondered why he was there and what happened to James Collier. They must have seen each other."

It was the clue Nat needed. Now for the proof. But how?

"By the way, your friend Button came yesterday with a message from Mr. Bacon and he is coming back today."

Nat waited for Button. He would tell Button the whole story. Not that he trusted him as a friend, but Button would think of some way to trap James Collier. If only it could be done before Nat left for Boxworth.

He could tell the minute Button arrived. Prisoners up and down the narrow, stinking hall called, pounded on the bars and pleaded, "Any message for me? There has been a terrible mistake. I am innocent, I swear. Tell your master."

Button's red hair glowed like a torch in the dark hall. He dodged the clutching hands and arrived at Father's cell out of breath.

"Nat, what are you doing here?"

"I'll tell you outside."

The message from Francis Bacon to Father was to have patience with God's secret darts.

"Then Mr. Bacon thinks Father is innocent?" Nat asked Button when they were outside.

"Of course. He never doubted it."

Button's lofty, know-it-all air exasperated Nat just as much as before. "Then why doesn't Mr. Bacon free Father?"

"He can't."

"Why not?"

"Because there's no proof that your father isn't guilty."

"James Collier is back of it all," Nat burst out. The story poured out, jumbled, hindside first—the new job as tutor to John Bois' six-year-old son, the planting of the St. Chrysostom papers in his bed, the actor and all the parts he had played, and how James Collier had not paid him. Finally, Nat told about the meeting James Collier attended, but he held back the clue Father had given.

Button caught on fast. "A Catholic! We'll turn him in and get a reward."

"With what proof?"

"Oh," Button sighed. "I forgot about that." Then he

65

brightened. "When do you have to go to Boxworth?"

"I'm starting today."

"Well, don't," Button said. "I have a great idea. The gossip at court says a new shipload of Catholic priests has just come in. This means they'll have to be hidden here and there all over the city."

What was Button getting at?

"My master has to direct a masque at court tonight, so I can slip out. You and I can keep watch near Sir Dudley's house and watch where James Collier goes. From what you have said, he'll be sure to go some place."

Nat could not see how that was going to give them the proof they needed, but the plan appealed to him. "Where will I go afterward?"

"You can come with me."

That night Nat waited for Button near Sir Dudley's house. He felt uneasy. What if someone from the household saw him? He was supposed to be on his way to Boxworth, staying at an inn after what should have been a day of riding a post-horse. Here he was, instead, back where he had been asked to leave.

Feeling more and more uncomfortable, Nat wondered where Button was. Could Button be playing a joke on him—on his gullibility? He remembered Button's mischievous streak. Was Button off at court laughing? Besides, what could be hoped for from their plan? They might see James Collier go into the nobleman's house, but what then? They should have alerted a constable. Too late for that.

Too late for anything. James Collier came out of the house, his hat low and his collar up. Someone stopped him. It was Button, asking for directions. James Collier made an impatient answer and stalked off.

66

Button hurried over to Nat.

"What did you ask him?" Nat demanded.

"How to find Sir Dudley Carleton's house," Button laughed.

"But why did you show yourself? If he sees you at the nobleman's house he will be suspicious."

"What if I say Sir Dudley sent me over with a message for him? He'll believe me, because he saw me before."

It was a brilliant idea, Nat had to admit. If James Collier thought Sir Dudley knew about his night trips, he would be sure to betray himself some way. Much heartened by Button's inventiveness, Nat led the way to the secret meetinghouse, but this time no sound came from the darkened rooms.

"Are you sure this is the right place?" Button asked.

Nat nudged Button to be quiet. The door opened and a man in priest's robes came out, followed by James Collier and two other men.

"It's a Catholic priest," Button whispered. "Never mind James Collier. A priest is worth lots more than just a secret Catholic."

A sudden thought shook Nat. If a priest were caught, he could be condemned as a traitor and die a traitor's death.

"It's no use. Let's go back," he whispered in his turn.

"Go back? We've just started. All we have to do is keep them in sight. We'll meet a night watchman sooner or later, and we can tell him. The night watchman can tell the constable and they'll catch him. Think of the reward we'll get."

It was not the time or place to argue. Nat followed Button, but his thoughts went around and around. Why should someone die just because he believed in

God in a different way? Didn't everyone have the same Scripture, the same Bible, whether it was in Hebrew, Latin, Greek, Italian, French, Spanish, or any other language? Maybe a word here or there might be translated differently, actual mistakes sometimes, but when found, they were corrected.

With reluctance, Nat trudged on through the darkness with Button. After all, he was tracking down a man who, if caught, could die as a result. James Collier was a different matter. As a secret Catholic, he had his own way of believing in God, but he had no right to have Father imprisoned on false charges. With this thought, Nat knew he would do whatever he could to bring about James Collier's arrest.

At the river Nat had a sudden fear that the men would take a boat. There would be no way to follow. The priest, however, seemed determined to walk.

At every set of stone steps leading to the water's edge, Nat listened for the rustle of oars, but the men ahead kept steadily on. James Collier looked back several times.

"Do you hear anything?" he asked.

"No. It's just the wind," one of the men said.

"But there isn't that much wind tonight. I'm sure I heard footsteps."

"Just an echo," someone else said.

"Or perhaps a night watchman."

A little later the men came to an abrupt stop, filed down stone steps to the water's edge. Their voices drifted upward.

"We'll wait for the boat here," James Collier said. "Now, Father Lambton, you joined us just tonight. You say you have been in England for several months. What have you found out?"

Before the priest could reply, one of the other men said, "Your name is Lambton, Father? Are you related to George Lambton?"

"Brother," the priest replied. "As you know, there is great distress among the priests in England. The money received is insufficient for those in prison. Furthermore, I understand from court gossip that the Spanish Ambassador has been reprimanded for allowing his priest to visit our prisoners."

"We must be careful about our visits to Newgate," one of the men said. "The keeper is to be punished severely for allowing Masses to be said in prison."

"But he is paid well," James Collier said.

"True, but if his fines are too heavy, or if he is replaced, we will be unable to carry out our great mission."

Father Lambton had a further warning. "The King is going to have the Spanish Ambassador's house watched to see who goes to Mass there, but not so openly as to attract notice."

Listening to the men below, Nat strained to hear the approach of a boat that would be carrying more Catholic priests into England. His previous sympathy gave way to quick anger. Why did Catholics insist on breaking the law of the land?

There was a sound on the water. The boat was coming in. "What will we do?" he whispered to Button. "We'd better find a night watchman, or better yet a constable."

"Wait! Wait! We have to make sure who is on the boat," Button said.

Nat could hear the steady splashing of oars, the creak of the gunwales, and a murmur of voices. Someone stood at the prow waving a dark lantern with a soft glow. As the boat touched the landing a loud command carried across the water. "I arrest you in the King's name."

Armed men sprang from the boat and leveled their pikes at the four secret Catholics. The priest stepped forward with utter calm. Nat could only admire his courage. So this was the way these men, trained in Europe, met attack! Nat, safe as he was, shivered in fear. James Collier, he could see, huddled against the stone steps just below Nat, and the other two men looked frozen to the spot.

"Bring the chains," the leader of the armed men ordered. The others turned to their boat. In a sudden burst of action, three of the Catholics dashed, scrambled, and clawed their way up the steps.

The King's men shouted, "Stop! In the King's name."

Footsteps clattered in the night. The three Catholics ran in different directions. Dogs started barking. The King's men raced after the Catholics, shouting in vain for them to stop. Shutters of houses opened. People in nightcaps looked out, muttered, and closed the shutters again.

The priest waited, making no attempt to escape.

"Who are they?" the leader asked the priest.

"I cannot give their names."

A strange answer, Nat thought, still amazed that the King's men had passed Button and himself without a second glance. Why didn't the priest say, "I don't know their names." The priest had given his answer in a tone of voice that implied he did not know, yet that was not what the words said.

"You surely know the penalties laid on those who are Catholic priests?"

"I am aware."

In a sudden burst of action, three of the Catholics dashed up the steps. Their footsteps clattered in the night.

"What were you waiting for here?"

"A boat," the priest said.

"Such talk will do you no good. It would be better for you to tell us the names of your companions, first of all. At your trial I can ask for the mercy of the court, saying you cooperated."

The priest folded his arms. "I cannot say more than I have."

"Your God will have to protect you then."

The King's men came back panting and cursing. "They got away."

Instead of looking pleased, the priest looked up the stone steps with a frown. "That is not what I intended."

"What's that you say?" the leader exclaimed.

"It's not at all what I had in mind," the priest said in such totally different voice that all the King's men looked at him in astonishment.

Nat understood first. The priest was not a priest at all. He was the actor, the one James Collier had not paid.

"Then you are the one who warned us about these Catholics in the first place."

"Yes," the actor sighed, "but it did not come out the way I planned. But I'll give you the name of one of the men—James Collier, secretary to Sir Dudley Carleton. I hope you catch him. He never paid me."

Button beckoned Nat. "Let's go. You'll stay with me tonight. There is nothing more we can do."

Loose ends, Nat thought. Would anything ever be solved?

7

SHAPING UP

That night in Button's room at Francis Bacon's house, Nat talked of rising early and hiring a post-horse for his journey.

"Why go so soon? A day or two or even three won't make that much difference, will it?" Button asked. "Does anyone in Boxworth know you're coming?"

"No. It all happened so fast."

"I'm sure John Bois won't send a fast messenger ahead of you to announce you're coming to Boxworth,"

Button laughed. "John Bois had to sell his library one time to pay off his wife's debts." Button knew bits of information about all of the Bible translators. "He doesn't have money for special messengers."

John Bois would be well paid for his work on the St. Chrysostom book, Nat reflected. There just had to be some justice in the world. As for leaving London, Nat admitted that he did not want to leave just yet. "I'll have to keep hidden."

Button shrugged. "That's easy. This is a large house. Just stay out of the way."

Nat agreed, but guilt rode on his shoulders like a heavy cloak. Should he be hiding like a criminal? That reminded him of James Collier. "There is one thing we can prove right away. Did James Collier go back to Sir Dudley's?"

"No," Button reported later. "He never showed up at all."

"Did you tell anyone about last night?"

Button shook his head. "No proof," he grinned.

Maybe I should go back, Nat thought. He liked being with Sir Dudley in the midst of important work, but there was no chance to study. In Boxworth as tutor, he could review Latin and Greek, as well as continue the study of Hebrew. John Bois would want his son to be prepared for college. It was time for Nat to think of college, too. Not that he would be able to enter Cambridge at the age of twelve, like Francis Bacon. Nat was already two years past that age.

"You can't go back to Sir Dudley's," Button warned. "You'd have to have a good reason, and you certainly couldn't tell about last night. But," he added, "you can tell my master, only it has to be at just the right time." Francis Bacon often worked many hours at a stretch.

74

He had a weak stomach and had to be careful of what he ate. "Sometimes he sleeps in the afternoons, or takes walks, or goes on horseback, or bowls."

The right time came. "He's walking in the garden," Button told Nat. "He'll see you now."

They found Francis Bacon pacing beside the wall. Of medium height, his hazel eyes gleamed above a neat mustache and beard. "Young men stir more trouble than they can quiet," he said after he heard the story of James Collier's flight.

"But we were just trying to find proof," Nat protested.

"If a man be thought secret, it invites discovery," Francis Bacon admitted. "But some affairs require extreme secrecy." He dismissed Nat and Button with a wave of his hand.

"What did he mean about secrecy?" Nat asked Button afterward.

"Everybody at court knows who he really is," Button said. He waited as if to hear Nat ask, "Who?"

Instead, Nat asked, "Is there gossip at court about him?"

"It isn't gossip; it's the truth. In the first place, my master wasn't provided for in his father's will, and do you know why?"

"No." Button should know better than to ask a question like that. Nat had never been around court life.

"Because Nicholas Bacon wasn't his father, that's why."

"Then who was?"

"Queen Elizabeth's husband, the Earl of Leicester."

Nat bristled. How could Button tell such outrageous lies?

"She was married secretly and had two sons."

Nat did not believe a word of this, but curiosity got the better of him. "Who was the brother?"

"The Earl of Essex."

"But he couldn't be," Nat exclaimed. "Queen Elizabeth had him executed. Why would she murder her own son?"

"He was going to overthrow the government. It's a long story." Button did not explain further. "Did you know one of the Bible translators was with Essex at his execution?"

Perhaps that was the truth, Nat thought. It must have been John Overall. Queen Elizabeth had heard him preach many times. Strange how people were interconnected with each other and with events in history. John Overall had gone to Hadleigh Grammar School and St. John's College at Cambridge with John Bois.

"No, it wasn't Overall. It was William Barlow," Button said. "And Lord Burghley made him preach in St. Paul's churchyard about Essex's treason."

That had the ring of truth, but not that wild gossip about Francis Bacon being the son of Queen Elizabeth. How could Button believe such nonsense? If she had been secretly married, why didn't she say so?

Button had an answer for that. "Because being unmarried meant a lot of kings wanted to marry her, and she kept them dangling and that way England kept out of wars."

Nat had one question that would put a stop to such talk. "Where's the proof for even one thing that you've said?"

Button took Nat to St. Martin-in-the-Fields Church to see the birth register. "Look at all the names on the page for January 25, 1560."

76

Nat looked at the list and discovered Francis Bacon's name. "So he was born on that day. What does that prove?"

"Didn't you notice that it said 'Mr. Francis Bacon'?"

For the first time, Nat noticed the *Mr.*

"None of the other boys' names have *Mr.* in front of the names."

"What does that prove?" Nat asked.

"That he is of royal blood. Only royal decree could change the way birth registrations are made."

Everyone at court knew the story, Button declared, and they knew why it was a state secret. Maybe that explained what Francis Bacon had said. Some affairs need extreme secrecy.

"If you stay around the court, you learn a lot of things that no one else knows," Button told Nat. "I could tell you much more about my master and all the writing he has done."

Nat remembered Button saying that Francis Bacon had paid someone to pretend to be the author of some of his works. "I don't want to hear any more court gossip. I'm going to Boxworth." Life in the country would be simple there. No tall tales there would strain his belief—above all, no secrets. Maybe by riding hard he could catch up most of the lost time he had spent with Button.

Button's last story was about the fast trip a rider had made after Queen Elizabeth's death. Button said the man rode four hundred miles from London to Edinburgh in sixty hours to be the first to tell King James the news and thus gain favor at court.

At Cambridge Nat turned in his post-horse without having made any kind of riding record, he thought with a grin. He shouldered his bundle and walked across the fields to the village of Boxworth, almost hidden by trees. He asked a housewife where John Bois lived.

"Look for the square tower of the church. The rector's house is nearby." She pointed toward a thick grove of trees.

Nat walked on, thought he saw the church tower, and discovered at a turn of the path that it had disappeared. He would have to ask someone else. A half-open door of a cottage invited him. He peered in and saw an old man at a table with open books within arm's reach. The old man wore the long black robes of a scholar. A black skull cap rode on top of his shaggy gray hair. His deep-set blue eyes twinkled under thick eyebrows.

"Come in, my boy, come in." The old man gestured to a stool. "My name is Daniel."

Nat wanted to ask the way to John Bois' house and be on his way, but it seemed impolite. "I'm Nathaniel Culver."

"Ah. Your father is one of the translators for King James, is he not?"

"Yes." Nat hesitated. Better not say Father was in jail. Too much explaining. "Are you one of the translators, too?"

"No. I was not chosen, although I must point out I am qualified." Daniel leaned back in his chair. "They feared my knowledge."

"Why would anyone be afraid of knowledge?" His own question annoyed Nat.

"Mine is a secret knowledge."

Nat sighed. Hadn't he just come from a place where secret knowledge—if true—could change history?

"I have studied the cabala," Daniel went on.

The word sounded mysterious but fascinating. "What kind of knowledge is that?"

"Oral tradition."

Nat had never heard of such a thing. "You mean it is passed down by word of mouth for thousands of years?"

"Yes," Daniel said. "Many people think it is forbidden knowledge. That is not true, but it is hidden from the unprepared." He reached for a quill pen and wrote four Hebrew letters, IHVH, and showed them to Nat. "Pronounce the word." He added, "In English."

"I can't."

"Why not?" Daniel asked.

"There aren't enough vowels."

Daniel tapped the letters with the end of his pen. "These four letters to the Hebrews stood for the name of God. They believed that if these letters were pronounced correctly God's power could be invoked." He asked Nat to pronounce the letters in Hebrew.

"Yod-heh-vau-heh," Nat said.

"What do the translators for King James call *God* in this new translation?"

"Why, just *God*, I suppose," Nat said.

"No, no. I mean in the Old Testament."

Nat racked his brain. "I guess it's *Jehovah.*"

"Ah, I thought so," Daniel said. "Why isn't it *Jehovah* in the New Testament?"

Nat had never heard of such questions. "I don't know."

"That is the difficulty with translating Scripture, getting away from the power of God."

Nat waited. There was nothing he could say to a remark like that.

"What are the translators doing about the vowels?" Daniel went on.

"What do you mean?" Vowels were *a, e, i, o, u.* What was the problem?

"How can anyone translate the vowel *a* into writing," Daniel asked, "when it is not spoken but breathed out." He breathed out a quick, silent *hah.* "In Latin it is called *spiritus,* the divine breath, but the mystery of the divine breath is lost in translation."

Excitement stirred Nat. "Is that why there is an oral tradition?"

Daniel nodded.

"But not everyone would understand about the power of God," Nat said. "They would be afraid."

Daniel nodded again. His blue eyes twinkled with approval. "That is why they are afraid of the cabala. Mystery teachings are not for everyone." He put his fingertips together. "They are for those with eyes to see and ears to hear."

That sounded like secrets of a different kind. If people knew about the power of God and how to arouse that power, they might use it the wrong way.

Lost in thought, Nat almost did not hear Daniel ask him what *yod* meant.

"Do you mean *God?*"

"No, I mean *yod.*" Daniel explained the word that was so much like *God.* "It means that which is, that which was, and that which will be. How many letters in the Hebrew alphabet?"

"Twenty-two."

"Did you know each letter has a *yod* in it some place?" Daniel asked.

Nat looked at him in astonishment. Such an idea had never occurred to him. Daniel explained that the alphabet came from the Chaldeans. "The Flame Alphabet, it's called. Yod means the open hand, the hand of God that shapes all things."

The old man's talk aroused a deep yearning in Nat to learn more, to understand more. He wondered how many more secrets there were in the mystery teachings. How much there was to learn. He saw Daniel watching him, as if waiting to tell him more.

"Who was Adam?"

Everybody knew that. "The first man on earth," Nat said. Really, that question was just too simple.

"There is a deeper meaning, Nathaniel."

How could that be? The first man was the first man.

"Adam is all men," Daniel said.

Annoyed, Nat retorted, "One man can't be all men."

Daniel smiled. "That's a mystery, isn't it? But the Bible is a mystery. That is why it is so powerful to all people everywhere."

Nat thought about the strange statement about Adam. How could the first man be all men? Did the translators of the Bible know that? Was that a mystery teaching?

"Nathaniel, what do you know about the Book of Revelation?"

"Isn't it a vision of some kind?"

"Yes, but what about?"

Nat remembered something about the seven cities of Asia, because when he heard about them he wanted to travel to those countries and see those cities.

"The seven cities of Asia are in you."

Nat jumped up, frightened. What nonsense was Daniel talking? Everyone knew there were cities in the world with those names, and one took boats and horses to visit them.

"The seven cities of Asia are in everyone."

Something impressive in the old man's voice kept Nat from running out of the cottage that very minute. Daniel must be out of his mind.

"I see you are frightened. That is always the way with something new," Daniel said. "Perhaps I should have waited a little, prepared the way." He reached under the table and pulled out a dulcimer, strummed the strings for a moment and began to sing. From time to time he glanced at an open Hebrew Old Testament.

Nat listened, forgetting his fears. The words and melody soothed him. "What are you singing?" he asked after Daniel paused.

"One of the psalms."

"But how did you know what notes to sing?"

"It's printed right on the letters." Daniel showed him tiny dots and little marks that looked like the letters *v* and *s* on their sides.

"Do you mean people sang the Scripture?"

Daniel nodded. "That is a fact your translators, I think, do not consider." He put the dulcimer away. "Think about the seven cities of Asia."

The soothing mood of the music left Nat. Fear took its place.

"Perhaps you may experience them, as other chosen people have done."

Nat choked. "I don't want to be chosen." He fled.

8

AN ENGLISH TIMOTHY

Nat looked back at the cottage, unable to shake off his fear of Daniel's strange words. The door to the mystery teachings stood halfway open. Would the old scholar call Nat back? Nat stared, longing to hear more of the Bible secrets and yet terrified. Besides, how could he be sure Daniel spoke the truth? An odd thought occurred to Nat. Was Daniel's door halfway open or halfway closed? Which was the truth?

Nat went on, bothered by his thoughts. On a village

footpath he made a sharp turn and saw ahead the square tower of the church. A little farther on he followed a winding path to the parish house.

He knocked on the door. A girl opened it. She was a little younger than he, with a saucy, uptilted nose, brown eyes, and light brown hair straggling from under her tight cap. Her sleeves were rolled to the elbows. She wiped her hands on her long, white apron, narrow at the waist.

Nat found himself tongue-tied. He had not expected to be met by a girl. In confusion, he jerked off his cap and stared at his feet.

"Well, speak up," the girl said.

"Reverend Bois—"

"He's not here," she interrupted. "He's in London. And stop staring at your feet."

"I know he isn't here. I—"

"Oh, then, you're the new Timothy."

"No, I'm Nathaniel Culver."

The girl burst into laughter. "You don't know your Bible, do you?"

"Yes, I do. I know it in Latin, Greek, and I've started it in Hebrew." Nat was going to add that he even knew a little French.

"You'd better read the Bible in English after Father and the others finish translating it." The girl's face brightened in good-natured mockery. "When it's published you can find out who Timothy is."

Nat burned with embarrassment. Of course he knew who Timothy was. The girl had just caught him off guard. St. Paul's Timothy was the young man whose name was a book of the Bible. How could he have been so stupid? He would have to be wary around this girl.

"I'm Mary Bois," she announced.

Here was his chance to get even. "You mean Mary Wood, don't you?"

Her brown eyes snapped. "I ought to know my own name."

"Well, it means *wood* in French."

Mary giggled. "You caught me on that one. Father teases us about our name. And do you know, Mother's name was *Holt* before she married Father, and that means *wood* in Dutch. What's your name? I mean what does it mean?"

"Dove-cote," Nat said. "My grandparents kept doves in Devon."

"Come in, Nat Dove-cote. You can't stand out there all day. I'll show you where you and all the other Timothys sleep."

"How many others are there?"

"Just you, at present, but there have been lots of other poor boys here."

Nat flinched. "I'm not a poor boy. I'm to be a tutor to your brother."

Mischief gleamed in Mary's eyes. "Which one? There's William. He'll be two next June. Robert will be one in May."

Nat stammered, "But I understood the one I'm to tutor is six years old."

A little boy came up behind Mary, clung to her skirt, and peered at Nat. The boy's hair under his cap was cut above his ears round as a wooden dish. He watched Nat's every move.

"This is John Two," Mary said.

"John who?" Nat was not sure he had heard correctly.

"The first John died," Mary explained, "so this one is

John Two. Father's name is John, too." She burst out laughing. "I mean Father's name is also John." She bent down and whispered to John Two, "Take off your cap and bend your knee."

John Two stood unmoving. Mary sighed. "I'm trying to teach him manners. But if you're his tutor, you can do it."

Nat found himself even more tongue-tied than before. He had no idea what to say to a child. He put his own cap back on, and Mary laughed.

"You'll never set an example that way. You'll have to learn some manners yourself if you live here. Father will see to that."

"Who's out there, Mary?" a woman called from an inner room. "Is it the candlemaker?"

"No, Mother. It's one of Father's Timothys."

Mrs. Bois came out, smiling a welcome. Taller than Mary, she was dressed the same—in a long dark skirt, a white apron, and with her hair hidden in a tight cap. A pouch dangled at her waist. Nat knew it contained what all housewives carried around with them— thread, scissors, and keys.

"Your husband asked me to be a tutor," Nat introduced himself.

Mrs. Bois sighed, hugged John Two, and sent him after his hornbook. "I'm afraid you'll have a hard time of it. John Two is not a scholar like his father. My husband had read the Bible through when he was five and could write Hebrew at the age of six. At the university he was considered very early summer fruit."

Not quite sure what Mrs. Bois meant, Nat glanced at Mary.

"Father was only fourteen when he entered Cambridge," she explained.

86

Someone knocked. It was a poor man of the church. "Please, Mrs. Bois, your husband said I was to come and get my free gift. He said I was to demand it as a debt, but I cannot do that."

"Yes, I know. It's quite all right. It's just my husband's way. I have the money here." Mrs. Bois opened the pouch at her waist and handed the man some money.

"Thank you, thank you, and may God bless you and your family." After more thanks, the man left.

Another man came with a bill for John Bois.

"My husband is in London. He'll be back this week or next," Mrs. Bois explained.

"Does he know how much debt he's in?"

John Two came in, swinging his hornbook by its cord.

"Debt? Oh, dear, not again. I've tried so hard to be careful."

Wide-eyed, John Two looked from his mother to the bill collector.

"My husband is expecting to be paid soon for work he is doing for Sir Henry Savile."

The bill collector grunted. "Sir Henry Savile, eh? He's rich, I hear. I'll be back. Good day to you, Mrs. Bois."

Mrs. Bois sighed and closed the door. "Money is the root of all evil, I do believe."

"Not money, Mrs. Bois," Nat ventured. "It's the love of money, the Bible says."

Mrs. Bois agreed and added that it was not her love of money that made the debts. "We usually have several students to feed. Some come for miles without having broken their fast."

"But Mother," Mary said, "Father did the same

when he was a boy going to school, two miles each way."

"Your father is used to fasting. Even now he does it quite often. But the food is much dearer these days. Still, I confess I don't know how the money goes."

Another visitor announced himself. "It's the candlemaker, ma'am, come to make the candles."

"Mary, come help me get the kitchen fats ready. Nathaniel, you might as well take charge of John Two. You can go into the study and help him with his reading. When it's time for his Hebrew lesson, he is to go to an old scholar here in the village. It will be better if you stay with him during the lesson. John Two knows the way."

The candlestick maker followed Mrs. Bois and Mary to the kitchen. In the study, Nat placed two stools near the window and discovered John Two had left the room. Nat found him in the passageway to the kitchen holding his nose. "The yellow candles don't smell good. I wish we had candles with cotton wicks. But candles are better than rushes dipped in grease. Mother doesn't like them at all. Candles cost more, though."

In the study, John Two folded his arms across his hornbook and refused to sit on a stool. "This isn't the way Father does it."

"What does he do?"

"First, he prays. He starts everything with a prayer."

"Then we will, too," Nat said. "Say the Lord's Prayer with me."

Afterward, John Two announced, "That's not the way Father does it."

"How does he do it?"

"He gets down on his knees on the bricks," John

Two explained. "He says you ought to feel a little pain when you pray. It reminds you that God is there."

"Suppose you kneel on the bricks, then," Nat said.

"No. They're too hard. When I'm bigger, I'll do it the way Father does."

Nat straightened the sheets of words under the thin, translucent cover of horn. "Let's study this together."

"That isn't the way—"

Annoyed, Nat tried not to show it. Had he been such a pest when he was little? "How does your father do it?"

"He stands up when he studies. When he was at Cambridge in the summer, he used to study from four in the morning until eight at night."

"Would you like to study that long?"

"Oh, no!" John Two exclaimed.

"Or stand up now and study?"

"No. I'm too little. When I grow up, I'll do it the way Father does." John Two moved his stool away from the window. "Father never studies near a window."

Nat moved the stools to the other side of the study. He pointed to the alphabet on the hornbook and asked John Two to recite.

"I want to look at Father's Bibles." John Two showed Nat the special cabinet containing Bibles and pulled out a Coverdale Bible of 1535, a thick, heavy book almost as long as Nat's forearm. John Two quickly found the pictures showing Samson breaking the temple columns and David ready to hurl a stone from his slingshot at Goliath, who was looking skyward. There was a picture of the Apostle John, looking skyward, too, and writing in a book. And also one of an eagle with wings outspread.

"Does your father want you to look at these Bibles?" Nat asked, a little uneasy. He could see that John Two had a mind of his own, even if it did not seem the scholarly type.

"Oh, yes." John Two brought out a Matthews' Bible of 1537, about the same size as the Coverdale Bible. Its pages were yellow, with red and black type in two columns. There were marginal notes, and John Two showed Nat an occasional tiny printed hand pointing out special passages.

"I like the picture of Adam and Eve best," John Two said. There were monkeys, deer, elk, rabbits, and birds in the picture, with God in a cloud and fish in the water. One page had fifteen little pictures all around the edges.

"Will Father's new Bible have pictures?" John Two asked.

"I don't know." Nat had never thought of how the King James Version of the Bible would look. He remembered the translators had agreed this version should not have marginal notes or comments, so that God's Word would stand alone.

Mary came in. "Has John Two read from the hornbook yet?"

Something in her tone made Nat's cheeks burn. What kind of tutor was he if he could not get his pupil to recite? "No. We were looking at the Bibles."

"Looking at them? That isn't reading."

"Well, no. We were looking at the pictures."

Mary put her hands on her hips. "What a fine Timothy you are."

Nat burned and silently vowed to teach John Two how to read.

"Are we going to prison?" John Two asked with a

suddenness that made Nat jump.

"Whatever gave you that idea?" Mary asked.

"We're in debt. The man said so."

Mary sent John Two out to the kitchen to see how the candle making was coming along. John Two bounced out of the room with a triumphant glance at Nat.

Mary told Nat how her mother years ago had not known how to manage a house. "Father had to sell his darling."

"His what?"

"His darling—his Greek books. He had almost all the Greek authors in his library. Catherine—that's our maid—says Father was going to leave Mother and travel to other countries, but he has never said a word about that. Catherine says it's like a broken bone. If it is well set, it is the stronger for having been broken."

So John Bois had his troubles, too. Of all the translators, Nat would have thought mild John Bois had the mildest life of anyone. Sir Henry Savile had lost his only son; Richard Thomson was a drunkard; Nat's own father was in prison. Did everyone have some special problem in life? Hugh Broughton, who was not a translator because of his terrible temper, old Daniel, who knew too much to be a translator. How strange it all was.

"Father was going to be a doctor," Mary said.

"What happened?"

"Every time he read about a disease, he thought he had it." She told how one time her father really did have smallpox at just the time when he had to show up in person to receive a fellowship. Andrew Downes and others carried him wrapped in blankets and in his sickbed to the place where he had to be.

91

That was another strange thing. Nat remembered the bitter words Andrew Downes had used against his former pupil. He had sounded jealous because Sir Henry Savile had preferred John Bois' notes on St. Chyrsostom.

"I wish they'd finish translating the Bible," Mary went on. "It has been almost four years—no, longer than that." She sighed. "It seems like forever. Every week Father would go to Cambridge, and now he's in London. We were hoping John Two would learn to read and surprise Father by the time he comes back."

"I haven't been around children," Nat said, "but I'll do my best. Though I can't see why he should start Hebrew." Or did he mean that he did not want to take John Two to Daniel's? How could Hebrew letters be taught to a boy who was having such a hard time with English?

John Two returned, edging into the room with a sly glance at his sister. She laughed, kissed him under his ear, and turned him over to Nat. "He knows the alphabet. Just get him to read."

After she left, Nat picked up the hornbook. Little John looked so downcast, Nat had to smile.

"I can read," John Two announced. He picked out a sentence.

"Ah, so; he is my foe," he read in a painfully slow voice.

"Do you know what that means?" Nat asked John Two.

"No."

Just as well, Nat thought. If English was so hard to understand, what would Hebrew be like? Would old Daniel tell a little boy some of the secret truths of the Bible?

9

THE POWER OF THE WORD

When it was time for the Hebrew lesson, John Two chattered all the way to the cottage. Too bad he couldn't be as lively learning English, Nat thought.

Daniel welcomed them, waved aside Nat's stammered explanation, and showed John Two the first letter of the Hebrew alphabet.

"There's a secret about *aleph.*" Daniel bent forward, his finger to his lips.

John Two sat alert, eyes wide.

"You have to breathe the first letter, not pronounce it." Daniel breathed the 'hah' and John Two echoed, 'Hah—hah—hah," with enthusiasm.

"The divine breath, the beginning," Daniel reminded Nat.

For the second letter, *beth*, Daniel drew a house. "What is this?"

"A house." John Two drew one. He held it up proudly.

"In Hebrew *beth* is a house. What can you do in a house?"

John Two thought of several things. "You can go in and out and sleep and eat there."

By the time Daniel explained a few more Hebrew letters as a door, a window, a nail, a sword, a field, and even a snake, Nat saw that John Two learned fast. Why didn't all teachers use this method?

Nat thought about the power of words. Some words carried truth better than other words. There were door-words, nail or sword-words, snake-words, and then the mixtures, when groups of letters formed still other words. Every word had its own special power. But the *Word* was God.

"There's only one truth, isn't there?" Nat blurted.

Daniel nodded.

"Then why don't the Catholics and Protestants see it?"

Daniel gestured toward John Two, busy drawing first a coiled snake and then an uncoiled one striking upward. "His truth is as much as he can grasp."

"Then that's why the Bible has stories?" Nat felt the excitement he had felt before. "They are for people who can't grasp more." A new name came to him. "If you knew the meaning of the letters in the Bible

94

names, you would know how God shows Himself to people."

Daniel smiled. "These are the mystery teachings."

"Then that's why one man's meat is another man's poison. God's truth is greater and contains both." Exhilarated by his discoveries, Nat could see he was learning just like John Two.

John Two still had trouble learning manners. At the supper table later Mary had to remind him to put his cap back on. "Do you want hair to fall on your plate?"

During the meal someone came to the door. Nat heard words that sounded familiar.

"I've come to be paid my debt."

Mrs. Bois paid him. "It's quarterly time," she explained to Nat. "My husband has invited some of the poor to ask him every quarter for money, and to demand it as a debt, lest he forget."

Nat could understand why Mrs. Bois would find herself in debt, running short of money because she was giving so much away under her husband's instructions.

"I don't know how we'll make out until your father returns from London," Mrs. Bois murmured to Mary. "I understand he will be earning thirty shillings a week. You know he did not receive anything for his translating except the honor of doing it for King James."

"You could sell some of his books, like his Greek Testament. He knows it by heart," Mary suggested.

"Oh, don't say such a thing, though I do hate a debt."

The next morning Nat was up early for the usual cold breakfast. There was no time for ovens or fires to heat up food. Afterward, John Two bounded into the study. He removed his cap, just as he would before his own parents. Mary must have taught him manners, Nat thought.

"I don't want to learn my letters," John Two announced.

Nat groaned. Wasn't there going to be a carry-over from the Hebrew lesson?

"I want to see the Bible pictures, like David throwing the rock at Goliath, like this." John Two swung the hornbook around his head.

Nat ducked. "What will you be able to read for your father when he comes back?"

John Two sobered. "I'd better learn something, or Father won't give me his daily blessing. Once when I was naughty he wouldn't speak to me for two days."

" 'Laborare est orare,' "Nat quoted.

"You're speaking Greek."

"No, that's Latin."

"What does it mean?"

"To work is to pray."

John Two settled down and wrote his letters. Mary brought in a supply of ink, freshly made. She persuaded Nat to show her how to make some of the Hebrew letters. Two men arrived and talked with Mrs. Bois. They looked into the study.

"These books are worth a fortune," one said.

Mrs. Bois promised money to pay the bills as soon as her husband returned.

The door closed behind the men and Nat heard her say, "Whatever shall I do? Where can I get the money this time?"

It was a question without answer.

"Why does it take the translators so long?" Mary

asked with a sigh. "Why don't they hurry up and finish?"

"They have to compare their words with the earlier translations."

"I heard Father say there were errors in the earlier Bibles. How can they know it's God's Word if there are errors?"

The question stumped Nat. He thought of the ways errors could be made—in translating, in copying, in printing.

"Why doesn't God tell them what to put down? Why doesn't He carve it on golden tablets, the way he did for Moses?"

Nat tried to answer. "Maybe there's another meaning to those tablets. Maybe there weren't actually golden tablets."

"It says so, right in the Bible, so there."

How could he explain something that was still so new to him? The Bible had multiple meanings, and there was no way to tell Mary. "Translators have problems like whether to use the word *within* or *among*." Here was a way to make Mary understand. "Would you say, 'The kingdom of God is within you' or 'The kingdom of God is among you'?"

Mary thought a moment. "That's easy. It's 'among' because God's kingdom couldn't be inside a person."

"It has to be 'within' because there's a secret truth in those words."

"Prove it," Mary challenged.

Nat had to laugh. Here was this idea of proof coming up again. How could anyone prove anything? "If you had a toothache, could you prove it to me?"

"I suppose not. I could only tell you about it."

Nat waited. Maybe she would see something for

herself if she had time to think it over.

"Like Sir Henry Savile's wife telling him she wished she were a book."

"What's the point?"

"Oh, it's just that I remembered Andrew Downes telling Father about it. Andrew Downes laughed and Father didn't."

Sir Henry had pored over his books so much that his wife made that remark. "And then you'd have a little more respect for me," she had said after telling him she wished she were a book." Sir Henry had said, "Madam, you had best be a calendar and I could change you every year."

Mary giggled. "And his wife was very displeased." Another time, Sir Henry was ill. His wife said if he died she would burn the manuscripts on St. Chrysostom because they would be to blame for killing her husband. "And do you know what Father said to her? He said that would be a great pity. She asked who St. Chrysostom was and Father said, 'One of the sweetest preachers since the apostles' time.' "

"What did Sir Henry's wife say?" Nat asked.

"She said she would not for all the world burn those papers." Mary seemed to have forgotten about the choice of *within* or *among* in connection with the kingdom of God.

During the rest of the day John Two rushed about livelier than usual. Sometimes he played a kind of hide-and-seek with Nat. Even more puzzling, John Two went into the study on his own accord. After the noon meal, Nat heard a rustle in the study.

"What are you doing?" Nat asked. He could not imagine John Two studying on his own, even after Daniel's excellent teaching.

"Just looking at some books."

Nat heard less than truth in John Two's voice. What was this little boy hiding? Nat knew him well enough to know he was not telling the truth. "Out with it. What are you doing?"

John Two started to cry. "We're in debt."

"But that doesn't have anything to do with you." Or did it? Was John Two trying to shoulder a family burden?

"When those men were here, they said Father's library was worth a fortune."

A terrible suspicion came over Nat. What was John Two trying to say? He searched through the books. Were any missing? The grammars. Were they there? Thomas Linacre's Latin grammar was there. What about the Greek dictionary?

Nat grabbed John Two by the arm. "You sold that Greek dictionary belonging to your father. Where is the money?"

John Two muffled his sobs. "I don't have the money. The man said he was coming after the other book today."

"What other book?" Nat pawed through the books again. It must be the Hebrew grammar. "Where is it?"

"Upstairs in the clothes chest."

"Bring it here."

John Two protested. "But if we don't get money to pay our debts, Father will go to jail." He brought the book down, tears in his eyes.

Nat determined to keep John Two in sight, but Mrs. Bois asked him to look after the two babies with Mary during the marketing hours. Catherine, the maid, was sick. Mrs. Bois had to buy food.

A little later Nat heard hoofbeats. He raced to the

door in time to see a man riding off and John Two racing upstairs. Nat caught up with him. Mrs. Bois and Mary had just returned.

"You did it when I told you not to." Nat took the money.

"But I promised the man."

"You can't promise something that doesn't belong to you. Which way did he go?"

"Toward Elmsett, I think."

"We're going after him," Nat said.

"We can't. Mother is letting a neighbor use our horse. Besides, by the time you get the horse and saddle it, the man will be gone."

Nat pulled John Two along to the neighbor's, explained that they had to overtake someone, put John Two in front of him, and rode off bareback. They caught up with the man not far from the village.

"Sir, there has been a mistake about the books," Nat panted.

"What books? I know nothing about any books." The rider muffled his cloak tighter around him.

"Here is your money back. It was all a mistake."

The man flourished his riding whip. "Get out of my way. If you don't, I'll thrash you."

"You'll have to thrash me then. I can't go back without those books."

Something in Nat's desperation must have touched the man. "Give me the money then. Here are your books." He flung them on the ground and wheeled off.

Nat slid off his horse, picked up the books, and dusted them with his sleeve. He and John Two rode back without a word. Nat reflected on the power of no words at all. How was he going to explain all that happened? Would John Two be punished or praised?

"Sir, there has been a mistake about the books," Nat panted. "Here is your money back."

As they approached the house Nat saw a horseman dismount at the front door.

"It's Father," John Two shouted. "He's home!"

The next morning John Two took off his cap and bent his knee before his father. "Bless me, Father."

John Bois did not look up. Hadn't he heard? Nat shuffled his feet in torment. Fathers gave blessings to the household morning and night. Was John Two's father going to withold his blessing? Nat tried not to remember the painful scene about the books.

It was my fault. I shouldn't have let it happen—any of it. It was bad enough to be accused in London of stealing, even though Nat was sure everyone understood he had not done it, but to be tutor to a small child and have another almost-theft take place really hurt.

"I'll apologize," Nat told himself. He framed a little speech in his mind.

There was no chance the rest of the day. When John Bois studied, no one disturbed him. At prayers, he knelt on the bare bricks by the fireplace. When he read the Scripture, he uncovered his head. Afterward, there was no chance to say anything. Again Nat marveled. How strong words were that were not even spoken.

"You know he thinks the world of his books," Mary whispered in the hall.

"But John Two was trying to help out."

"I know, but Father is like that. It doesn't happen often, and Mother says the reasons are best known to himself. She says it's too hard for anyone to dive into." Mary smothered a giggle. "Father swam a lot when he was young. Maybe he did his diving then." She added, "He always either sits or walks an hour after he eats. Maybe you can talk to him then."

John Bois chose to walk. He took no one with him. Nat kept waiting for a chance to speak to him. Of course no one interrupted John Bois when he withdrew to "tend to his teeth," Mary explained. "He thinks it is very important."

John Two made no noise at all. It seemed to Nat that the whole family was waiting for something to happen to bring everything back to normal.

"Father has such good stories to tell," Mary said.

Nat had not told Mary about his own experiences in London. Now he found himself telling her about his father, James Collier, Button, and the actor. Mary and John Two listened in wide-eyed fascination. "I wish I could go to London," he said. "If only Father would forgive me, maybe he'll take me next time."

Silence wasn't going to work forever, Nat decided. He would ask forgiveness for his own part and for John Two also. If only he knew enough Hebrew! He believed in the power of those words. But he could use Greek. Every language must have its own power.

He approached John Bois just before bedtime and addressed him in Greek.

John Bois smiled. "Yes, my boy."

Nat apologized in Greek. To his relief, John Bois blessed him and the rest of the household. After that, no more was said about the almost-sold books. Had just words brought about the change—or the power behind the words?

10

THE OLD AND THE NEW

The whole household had been affected by John Bois'
silent treatment. Now that he was himself again,
everyone asked questions about London at the first of
the two daily meals he allowed himself. Nat's father
was out of jail.

"How did it happen?" Nat asked, excited and relieved.

James Collier never showed up as a witness, nor
had he returned to Sir Dudley's. Without more proof,

there was nothing Nat's father could be condemned for. And the actor, still bitter about not being paid for his professional work, confessed his part in planting the illegal books.

The mystery surrounding James Collier would probably never be cleared. Nat had not told anyone his deepest suspicion about James Collier, that he was not just a Catholic but a Catholic priest. A belief was not enough to prove anything.

"When will the new Bible be published?" Mrs. Bois asked.

Her husband explained that it was in the hands of King James. The King had been asking for months when he could expect the entire manuscript. Of the three completed Bibles, one from each of the three committees—Westminster, Oxford, and Cambridge—the final choice had been made by the little group who had been working for thirty shillings a week at Stationers' Hall.

"At last you've finally been paid something for all your years of work," Mrs. Bois sighed. "It isn't much, but it will help."

Her husband explained that in 1604, when the plan for a new translation of the Bible had first been made, the King's purse was empty. His expenses of one hundred thousand pounds that year had doubled from the previous year.

"How could his purse be empty?" John Two asked. "I thought kings were rich."

"They tax people," Mary said. "They get lots of money that way, but think of all the people they have to pay." On the other hand, she had heard how sick people paid in silver to touch the King, believing they would be cured.

John Bois remembered how the bishop of London did not think the Bible could be retranslated for less than a thousand marks, about seven hundred pounds.

"How much has it cost?" Mary asked.

No one could ever estimate the work the fifty-four translators had done, the thousands of hours put in over the years.

"I like the Geneva Bible best," Mrs. Bois said. "It's the household Bible of Britain." But she had to admit knowing that King James did not approve of the Bible published by a group of English exiles in Geneva, and the King's wishes had to be carried out.

"Will King James's Bible show how the psalms are to be sung?" Nat asked.

"Nathaniel, what makes you think you are supposed to sing them?" Mrs. Bois asked.

"The Hebrew has little marks in the letters that show you what notes to sing."

Mrs. Bois agreed they ought to be sung, but there was no way to indicate the notes in the English letters. Nat thought about that. There would be something lost, then, in this new Bible. Maybe that was the problem of all translating. Something is lost. Since he had begun to understand something about the multiple meanings of the Bible, he asked himself if these meanings would be lost in translation, or would the power of God's Word work anyway? For some people it would be as if someone handed them a sealed book to read, or like being at a well without a bucket.

John Two was more interested in his dinner than in the talk. "It's a feast day, isn't it? I smell gingerbread." Not only that, there was new wheat boiled with milk and sweetened with honey. "Frumenty!" John Two was ecstatic. "That's my most favorite food of all."

106

Not long afterward, John Two complained, "I don't feel well."

"Mary, get the rhubarb syrup," Mrs. Bois ordered.

John Two recovered quickly, in time to make the prayer at the end of the meal. His father left the house on his usual after-dinner walk. In a short time a man came to ask for food. "Your husband sent me," he told Mrs. Bois. "I told him I wasn't a beggar, and he said he knew that. He said, 'Charity's eyes must be open as well as her hands.' I said, 'What do you mean by that, Reverend Bois?' and he said, 'Charity must relieve necessity but not foster sloth,' and I agreed."

Word spread fast in the village that John Bois was back.

Neighbors asked advice, the poor came to his dinner table or received food. Parents asked John Bois to prepare their sons for further education. Nat found that he was not the only Timothy. He studied with those who came to the house, some on foot, others on horseback.

"Doesn't Daniel teach classes, too?" Nat asked Mary after John Two's Hebrew lesson with the old scholar.

"Oh, no." Mary looked astonished, as if he should know why.

"But he's a learned man." Nat sensed the reason why, but he wanted to know what Mary would say.

"Yes, but people are afraid of him. He has studied the—" Mary lowered her voice and put her finger to her lips.

Were people really that afraid of the cabala? How could they be afraid of something they knew nothing about? Was Mary so afraid she could not even say the word?

"He studied the what? Why did you stop and put

107

your finger to your mouth?"

Mary stamped her foot. "You're teasing me. You know very well why I stopped. I don't know why Father sends John Two there, except that John Two couldn't learn any Hebrew when Father tried to teach him, and now he's coming along very well."

"What about that word?" Nat persisted. "What was it that Daniel studied?"

"The cabala," she said, letting her breath out in a deep sigh.

"That's just a Hebrew word meaning 'to receive.' "

"It's secret knowledge, and people shouldn't have anything to do with it."

Some are chosen, Nat reflected, but he did not tell Mary that. He could smile now at how frightened he had been when Daniel called him chosen. It was being gullible again, believing his own fear to be the truth.

As the weeks passed there was no message from London as to when the new Bible would be out. It had not even been entered into Stationers' Hall, according to some neighboring ministers who had visited London and who now met in their customary way at first one house and then another to discuss their studies. Someone said the King's printer, Robert Barker, only shrugged when asked about the printing of the new version.

What was the delay? The whole manuscript, the one chosen from three complete manuscripts, had been turned over to King James. He was a fast reader. He had asked for the work to be completed months before the translators were able to do it. Of course no one could question the King's right to do as he chose. In fact, he could choose not to have the new version published.

"We shall just have to keep on using the Bishops' Bible," one of the ministers said when the group met at John Bois' house. "The last edition was in 1606."

Another minister joked, "Or else we'll have to use the Catholic Bible." The Douai Bible had been published only a few months before.

"It took the exiles only two years or so to put out the Geneva Bible," another said.

The men discussed the mystery of Whitchurch's Bible, how it was really Tyndale's, but after Tyndale had been burned at the stake for translating the Bible, his name could not be used.

For whatever reason, there was an unmistakable delay in the printing of the King James Version of the Bible.

While the Bois family and Nat waited for news of the printing, Sir Henry Savile himself arrived one day on horseback. With a flourish and with many flowery words of thanks, he presented John Bois with a copy of the St. Chrysostom book.

"Without your help, it would never have come to be," Sir Henry said with a tremor in his voice. "It has been my life's dream to see that the writings of the great church father should be properly set forth."

Nat could see Mrs. Bois twisting her hands under her apron. At last the hundreds of hours John Bois had spent on that work would be properly rewarded. Nat could almost see her mentally paying off every last household debt. He wondered how much money the work was worth, certainly hundreds of pounds.

"It took my fortune, just as I said it would," Sir Henry said. "There are more volumes coming, of course, but with all of the editing work done, the other volumes should be out within two years. Eight thousand pounds. Imagine. It's the joy of my life. More than anything else, it has helped ease the tragedy in my life."

Everyone understood that he meant the death of his son. John Bois had experienced such a death, too, his first son named John.

After a meal with the Bois family, Sir Henry left, waving his hand to the whole group.

Mary whispered to Nat, "Isn't he handsome? His skin is just like a woman's, so soft looking and white."

"You're just saying that because he's rich," Nat whispered back.

But where was the money for John Bois' work? Not a word had been said, only a book thrust into Bois' hands as payment.

"You must say something," Mrs. Bois implored. "How can he do this to you?"

But John Bois did not complain. He never received any money for his work on St. Chrysostom.

Not long after Sir Henry's visit, Andrew Downes rode over from Cambridge and stormed into John Bois' house. He towered over John Bois, and with his face redder than ever he let the whole household know why he was angry. John Bois' notes and not his had been used in the finished work. Sir Henry, Nat remembered, had favored John Bois' work even months before. Now it meant jealousy between teacher and student.

"I do not deserve this," John Bois said after Andrew Downes left, "but I am much bound to bless God for him." It was Downes who had revived Greek as a respected language at Cambridge University.

The Bible delay continued. John Bois decided to go to London and was willing to take John Two along for a first trip there, and Nat. John Two was delighted to learn that it was almost time for the Guy Fawkes celebration, and that he could join other small boys begging for pennies.

Nat felt an irresistible urge to look at the house where James Collier had visited so many months ago. On the pretext of letting John Two beg, Nat took him to the street that led to the secret meeting place. He lingered behind and watched John Two approach people.

"A penny for the guy. A penny for the guy." John Two held out his cap to people going into the house.

That was too dangerous, Nat decided. If Catholics were meeting there, they might not act with the good humor most people did. He noticed, however, that the people almost flung money to John Two.

One man hissed, "Go away," to John Two. Then he seemed to reconsider. "What's your name?"

"John Two."

"Is Two your last name?"

"No. It's Bois."

"Is your father a translator for King James?"

"Yes, sir." Pride shown on John Two's face.

"Ah, then you are coming with me," the man said.

Nat ran up. "Please, sir, he's just begging for pennies for Guy Fawkes' Day." Nat looked into the glittering eyes of James Collier. Instant recognition and alarm showed in Collier's face. He looked up and down the street.

"Where are they? Oh, don't look so innocent. I mean the constable and his men. They have been watching this house ever since my return. But God's will is greater than man's. No one is going to stop me from celebrating my first Mass on English soil." James Collier scooped up John Two and ran into the house. He called over his shoulder, "Keep the constable away if John Bois wants to see his son again."

There was no time to think about the threat. Nat had to rescue John Two. He darted inside. There were no servants in sight, not even a footman. From a large room down the hall Nat heard the murmur of voices. He could hear John Two crying in a small side room. Then the cries stopped. What was happening? Nat crept closer, hiding behind a chest of drawers in the hallway.

"What are you putting those funny clothes on for?" Nat heard John Two ask.

"I am serving God."

"Do you have to change clothes to do that?" John Two sounded quite at ease now.

Change clothes. Change clothes. The words rang in Nat's ears. Where had that been something meaningful in Father's life?

From the room James Collier had entered, a Catholic priest came out. In a flash Nat understood the mystery behind Father's visit in Paris. James Collier was the priest Father had seen. Why had he persecuted Father? *Because James Collier had thought Father recognized him as Dudley Carleton's secretary.* If Father had turned James Collier over to the authorities, once they both were back in England, it could have meant a traitor's death for Collier.

Nat heard footsteps close by. James Collier, the Catholic priest, grabbed Nat by the shoulder. "I knew you would come in. You and John Bois' son are coming with me."

"What are you putting those funny clothes on for?" Nat heard John Two ask.

"But we aren't spies, if that's what you were thinking," Nat pleaded.

"Why else would you be standing in front of this house?" James Collier gave Nat's shoulder a shake. "Sending a little boy to spy—" He pushed both boys toward the darkened room. "Nothing must interfere with mass. You will both sit quietly. Who knows? Maybe you will be converted." He found chairs for Nat and John Two.

A hush descended on the room. Whispers stilled. In spite of himself, not even wanting to, Nat felt a strange thrill. Here were people worshiping God in a way that was against the laws of the country where they lived. Could they possibly be right? Didn't the Bible include stories of people being persecuted for worshiping God? How could anyone know what was right?

The candles, the soft chanting, the altar with its white embroodered satin cover, the lifting of the cup, all of these made Nat sense a mystery in the worship of God.

When James Collier prayed, his voice shook with emotion. *He really believes what he is doing,* Nat thought. But how could he have done those other things, too? Then Nat thought of Dutch Thomson. How could a drunkard translate God's Word? How could Sir Henry Savile not pay for work done for him? How could Andrew Downes not forgive John Bois, when John Bois had done nothing to offend?

It was the story of Adam, old and ever new.

11

THE HIGH CALLING

During the service two men back of Nat whispered to each other.

"This is my first time," Nat heard the first man say. "Is this what is called a High Mass?"

"No, it's a Low Mass. Just one priest. No music. No incense."

James Collier, the priest, prayed several short prayers with fiery devotion.

"Why is he praying so much?" John Two whispered.

"Don't talk. Just watch," Nat answered.

"Why is he making all those motions with his hands?" John Two asked a little later. Nat nudged him to be quiet. He dimly understood the priest's ritual. It was to bring the presence of God into the room. No wonder people were ready to die for this experience.

At the end of the service the priest faced the audience. *"Ite, missa est,"* he said.

"That means, 'Go. You are dismissed,' " Nat told John Two.

As the people rose, the sound of many footsteps in the hallway made them pause.

"We are discovered," someone groaned.

"House search, in the King's name," a man shouted from the open door. Two armed men barred the way with their pikes crossed.

"Seize the priest," the leader ordered. Two other armed men stepped forward.

"Let us all go," a woman pleaded. "We'll pay the fine gladly."

"Yes, gladly," a man echoed. "I don't want to disgrace my family."

The leader of the armed men folded his arms across his chest and stared at James Collier. "Are you willing to pay the price?"

"Yes, yes, of course." He fumbled under his robes and brought out money.

The leader counted it in the hushed silence and nodded. In a voice that no longer sounded like an official's, he said in a mild tone, "Why didn't you pay me before?"

The actor! These were not the King's men, Nat realized, but the actor and his colleagues in guard uniforms.

116

The actor and his friends withdrew with a final word of advice to James Collier. "You have paid me in full, and I have no longer a grievance against you. Find another place for your illegal meetings. This place has been spied upon for a long time by one of the King's men."

It took a few minutes for people to realize the house search was a fake one. Without asking why an actor would put on such a scene, they dispersed. Nat grabbed John Two and hurried outside. To his surprise he saw Button Bushell leaning against a nearby stone wall.

"I saw it all," he said as he greeted Nat. It was as though they had parted only the day before. When he found out who John Two was, Button nodded understanding.

"Are you the spy the actor meant?"

Button nodded. "I just drop around from time to time. It's as interesting as one of my master's plays. Not that he knows I'm doing this on my time off," he added quickly.

All the excitement had tired John Two and he seemed glad to be returned to his father. Nat knew John Two would not tell about the afternoon's adventure unless asked.

"I wouldn't really turn James Collier in," Button explained later. "That would end all the excitement."

"Can you be a spy on another matter?" Nat asked.

"What do you want to know?" Button sounded patronizing.

"Why hasn't King James's Bible been published?" Nat told Button the translators had found out it had not been entered at Stationers' Hall.

"My master isn't through with it yet," Button replied.

"But the final manuscript was sent to King James, not to Francis Bacon."

"Do you mean you do not understand yet how things are done at court?" Button demanded. "But of course. You've been living in the country again."

Even though irritated now, rather than embarrassed, Nat kept on questioning. "Do you mean he is still reading it?"

"No. He's making it sing." Button explained how Francis Bacon, the most learned man of all the learned men in England, was changing a word here and there so that when read aloud, the Scripture sounded songlike. "My master always said he was born for the service of mankind. What greater service could he do than this?"

"But there were fifty-four scholars who translated," Nat argued.

"That's just it. One might have a short word and another a longer word meaning the same thing. Both could be right, but my master says the words have to sing to men's souls." Button admitted he did not know exactly what that meant, but Nat remembered what the old scholar Daniel had said about the power of words. In God's own book, the words chosen by man had to have that power.

Nat found out later that John Bois, alone of all the translators, had kept notes on some of the questions that had come up during the sessions of translating. Nat was permitted to look at them. He saw the neat pages of notes, written in Latin, Greek, and English. One note caught his attention. For Romans 14:5 John Bois had explained in Latin, "Let each one acquire for himself true knowledge from the Word of God, so that without doubt he may perceive the will of God."

In the notes there were many references to A.D.— Andrew Downes. One note in Latin spoke of A.D. sharply and violently holding to the interpretation of Augustine in a certain passage. None of the other notes spoke of Andrew Downes' grouchiness. How strange, Nat reflected, that the man who had brought Greek back to a high state at Cambridge University with the help of John Bois should now consider John Bois an enemy.

More important than the fact of two translators not on speaking terms, although that was not John Bois's doing, and more important than the fact that a drunken translator helped revise the new Bible was the question of whether King James approved of it.

"Do people know he passed it to your master?" Nat asked Button.

"No, and better that they should not know. My master wants his work to be as secret as that of the other translators. He has too many enemies at court envious of his high place. Of course, everyone at court knows who he really is."

Was Button going to start that again?

"I can see you don't believe me," Button said. "Don't you recognize truth when you hear it?"

Nat did not answer. It was not a matter of belief but of proof.

"How can you prove the author of the Bible is God and not man?" Button challenged.

There was such a thing as knowing the truth inwardly, but it was no use telling Button that. Since Button accepted the high calling of his master, Francis Bacon, there was hope that later on Button would understand God's truth to be different from what people ordinarily called truth.

12

THE WORD WENT FORTH

Nat promised to bring a copy of the Bible to Boxworth as soon as it came off the press. He would live there as a Timothy to complete his studies for entrance to Cambridge University.

"I'm going to college, too," Button told him.

"Where?" Nat asked in surprise. He thought Button would be Francis Bacon's servant for life.

"My master has his own college for inventions and experiments. He wants to found a school with workshops for the study of stones, plants, animals, medicine, astronomy, the tides, and heat and cold."

"Heat and cold?"

"Yes, like freezing chickens."

"What for?" Nat asked, puzzled by the scope of Bacon's ideas.

"To be used for food later on." Button explained his master wanted to know everything. "He says he was fitted for nothing so well as for the study of truth."

What was the truth about the delay in publishing the Bible? Button reported the gossip at court. People were saying the King did not like this version. "They say he thinks it is worse than the Geneva Bible and that the Bishops' Bible will still be used in churches," he told Nat's father.

"Father believed you," Nat reproached Button later on when they were alone. "Now he's asking all the translators within a day's ride of London to meet and discuss what's wrong with this translation. You've caused a lot of trouble. Why did you do it?"

"I thought your father would know the difference between gossip and truth," Button said airily. "You didn't believe it, did you?"

"No." Nat realized that somewhere along the way he had learned not to take anything for granted. Strange, though, that Button would pass on gossip yet never once hint at Francis Bacon's secret editing of the Bible manuscript. Then was his story about his master's royal birth true or not true? Would it make any difference in his service to mankind? Nat's silent answer was a firm *no*. He would not let that story bother him again.

"We can do no more," one of the translators said at the meeting Nat's father had called. He listed the previous Bibles that had been consulted—Erasmus's Greek text as revised by Stephanus and Beza, the Latin Vulgate, Hebrew texts, Luther's German and Olivetan's French Bibles, the Latin translations of Pagninus, Múnster, Castalio, and the Syriac New Testament.

One of the translators ventured a joking remark. "Now that the Catholics have their own Bible in English, maybe King James will prefer it."

Another translator took the remark seriously. "But the Douai Bible translated Latin word for word. It sounds wooden."

"Dr. Culver, what do you think?" someone asked thoughtfully.

"Perhaps we should have pondered our own insufficiency, as Coverdale says in the preface to his Bible," Father said, "but as Miles Smith and Thomas Bilson said in the preface to our version, 'Truly we never thought to make a new translation, nor yet to make of a bad one a good one, but to make a good one better, or out of many good ones one principal good one.'"

"Let no dog move his tongue against our translation," still another translator said.

"We subject ourselves to everyone's criticism," was the final word from the group.

Soon afterward the welcome news arrived. The Bible manuscript was being set up in type, four pages at a time, yet the mystery remained: the King James Version of the Bible was never recorded at Stationers' Hall. The final manuscript used for printing was never preserved.

Before Nat started for Boxworth with a copy of the new Bible for John Bois, he looked through it trying to find evidence of Francis Bacon's editing. In the

Bishops' Bible a passage had read, "Great love hath no man than this: that a man bestow his life for his friends." In the King James's Version it read, "Greater love hath no man than this, that a man lay down his life for his friends." Nat marveled at the music of the words. *They sang.*

He asked Father about changes in the printed version.

"I remember John Bois' translation of Hebrews 11:1," Father said. "His was 'Faith is a most sure warrant of things, is a being of things hoped for, a discovery, a demonstration of things that are not seen.' What does the new version say?"

Nat read the passage. "Now faith is the substance of things hoped for, the evidence of things not seen." That passage sang, too, along with many others changed by just a word or two from previous versions of the Bible.

Not everyone was pleased with the new Bible. Dr. Hugh Broughton, who had not been chosen as one of the translators because of his temper, criticized it immediately. "I had rather be rent in pieces with wild horses, than any such translation by my consent be urged upon poor churches." He added that the new version vexed him so much that he would like to see it burned.

As the preface said, "Whoever attempts anything for the public, especially if it pertains to religion and to the opening and clearing of the word of God, he sets himself on a stage to be gloated on by every evil eye. He casts himself upon pikes to be gored by sharp tongues."

But for most people, the new Bible spoke to their hearts.

123

Nat brought a copy of the 1611 Bible to Boxworth. As he unloaded it from the saddlebag of his hired post-horse, John Two ran out of the house.

"It's here! It's here! The King's book has come." John Two pranced around the horse trying to help Nat.

"Wait. Don't be so impatient. It's heavy. I'll carry it inside," Nat told him.

"I want to look at it."

"You'll have a chance, but first take the horse to the stable."

Inside, the whole family gathered around the table. Nat set the book down. The black letters of the three words, *The Holy Bible*, each word on a separate line, were followed by words of explanation in four different types. One sentence stood out: "Appointed to be read in churches."

"Look! There's Moses." John Two pointed to a bearded man at the top holding a double stone tablet. Another robed man in the picture held large keys. Still another was pictured writing in a book. There was a lamb with a nimbus around its head, and a pelican piercing its own breast while its young looked on.

"Let me open the book," John Two said. He opened it. Blank pages faced him. He turned the next page. It was blank, too. A third page was blank on one side but with a title page on the other.

"When does it start?" John Two asked. "I know some of the Bible by heart." He began to recite, "In the beginning. . . . "

"Wait," his mother said. "The translators have something to say to the readers."

John counted the pages of the translators' preface. "Eleven pages. When does the Bible start?"

The next pages contained morning and evening Bi-

124

"This is not the King's book," Nat said. *"This is the* King of kings' *book!"*

ble lesson suggestions. For each calendar month, the words *Sol in Aquario, Sol in Piscibus, Sol in Aries,* and so on, for the year, were in gold letters.

"Why?" John Two asked.

"That's when the moon changes," Mrs. Bois said.

One page of King James's Bible showed how to find the correct Easter date forever. The reader was told to find the Sunday letter in the uppermost line, guide his eyes downward in a certain way until he came across the date of Easter for that year.

John Two spotted an extra word at the very bottom of the page and asked why it was all alone.

"It's to guide your eye to the first word of the next page," Nat said.

The suggestion was made for the reader to read through the Old Testament once a year, except for certain books. The New Testament was to be read three times a year.

"When will the Bible start?" John Two asked plaintively.

The next seventeen pages showed genealogy, name after name. John Two was interested in the picture of Adam and Eve. "Look! There's the apple and the snake."

After an alphabetical table of all places mentioned in the land of Canaan and a map page, Genesis began. The Bible was printed in two columns with numbered verses with the first word of the next page added extra at the bottom.

John Two measured the Bible. It was longer than from his fingertip to his elbow, and almost as thick as his outstretched hand. "The King's book is big," he announced.

A sudden, strange feeling welled up in Nat as he

took the Bible from John Two. "This is not the King's book."

John Two appealed to his father. "It *is* the King's book, isn't it, Father?"

As John Bois' Timothy, Nat answered for him. "No, John Two, this is the *King of kings'* book!" He smiled at the puzzled expression on John Two's face. Some day he would understand.

The Author

Louise A. Vernon was born in Coquille, Oregon. As children, her grandparents crossed the Great Plains in covered wagons. After graduating from Willamette University, she studied music and creative writing, which she taught in the San Jose public schools.

In her series of religious-heritage juveniles, Vernon recreates for children events and figures from church history in Reformation times. She has traveled in England and Germany, researching firsthand the settings for her fictionalized real-life stories. In each book she places a child on the scene with the historical character and involves the child in an exciting plot. The National Association of Christian Schools honored *Ink on His Fingers* as one of the two best children's books with a Christian message released in 1972.